ON THE RUN

Cathy didn't know where she was driving. She didn't know where she was. She couldn't think back; she couldn't bring up a picture of two men sprawled on the pavement and the sound of gunfire ringing in her ears, or she'd start screaming. She had to drive, just *drive,* she had to get away . . .

Bad things just didn't happen to Cathy Hamilton. She knew small troubles and minor challenges and the everyday victories that went along with them. The car that wouldn't start, the credit card payment that got lost in the mail. Her world was uncomplicated and predictable, and she kept it that way almost by force of will. People did not call in the middle of the night to say that her brother had been in an accident. People didn't threaten her with guns or try to force her into strange cars or send her fleeing for her life down a strange highway in the middle of nowhere.

But the man in the red hat had pointed a gun at her. He had wanted to kill her. Two men were dead. She'd seen it with her own eyes. She hadn't wanted to, she hadn't meant to, but it had happened . . . and she had no idea what to do.

DONNA BALL
THE DARKEST HOUR

ZEBRA BOOKS
KENSINGTON PUBLISHING CORP.

ZEBRA BOOKS

are published by

Kensington Publishing Corp.
475 Park Avenue South
New York, NY 10016

First printing: July, 1992

Printed in the United States of America

Chapter One

There is something about the relationship between twins that no ordinary person can fully understand—nor, in fact, even believe, as much as he might want to. It was for that reason that Cathy Hamilton tried to keep her anxiety to herself, but she knew something had happened to Jack. She had known it since five-thirty that afternoon.

"Come on, Cath, you know how men are." Her friend Ellen tried to sound comforting but in fact came off as a little callous. "He got a better offer, that's all. He'll come breezing in here at three or four o'clock in the morning with this hangdog expression and some lame excuse, and—"

"I'll wring his neck," Cathy muttered.

Ellen grinned. "You'll throw yourself at his feet and forgive him anything, you know you will."

"Yeah," Cathy agreed reluctantly. "But first I'll wring his neck."

Against her will, her eyes moved across the crowded room, over the heads of laughing party-goers, toward the door that was open to the warm California night. Ellen followed her gaze and squeezed her arm sympathetically. They both knew that Jack would have called. If he possibly could have, he would have called.

Jack and the kids had been planning the trip to Canada for three months. It was the first real vacation Jack had had since his wife Lydia had left him — and her twin children — three years ago. He had asked Cathy to come with him, and she supposed she should have gone. Two five year olds on a camping trip were a lot for a man to handle, but she had genuinely felt it was important for Jack to spend some time with his children alone. And then there was the orchestra that she had worked so hard to organize all year, making its summer-season debut tonight. . . . She had been selfish, Cathy admitted now. She should have gone with him.

But she had talked to Jack only last night, and they were on their way home. They should have arrived by mid-afternoon today, at the latest. Where were they?

Jack had promised to be there in plenty of time for the concert. He would *never* have missed her concert, if he had had a choice. And the concert had ended two hours ago.

Glen Ellison, having overheard the last part of the conversation, turned toward Cathy with an encouraging lift of his glass. "Cheer up," he said. "Some of the best surprise parties I ever attended were those where the guest of honor didn't show up. And it's a great party. Of course," he added modestly, "we deserve it."

Cathy smiled, not because anything Glen had

said was funny, but because he always had that effect on her: his natural warmth and easy manner relaxed her whether she wanted to relax or not. An accountant by day and a virtuoso—for Lynn Haven, that was—double bassist by night, Glen was single, fairly good looking, and considered by most to be one of the few good catches left in Lynn Haven. Cathy liked him in spite of all that, and in spite of the fact that he had never abandoned the effort to try to make more of their relationship than there could ever be.

And he was right about two things—it was a good party, and they did deserve it. The party had a two-fold purpose: to surprise Jack with a welcome home birthday party, and to celebrate the newly formed Lynn Haven Orchestra's first concert of the season. The concert—Bizet's Symphony in C and Bach's Concerto in D for Two Violins—had been a resounding success. For Cathy, in fact for all of them, it was the culmination of a three-year-old dream, one she had almost given up hope of ever having come true.

There had been a time when her dreams were much bigger—the London Symphony, the New York Philharmonic—but long ago she had learned the futility of allowing her reach to exceed her grasp. She was content to teach music at the local high school and, tonight, to have made her debut as concert mistress of Lynn Haven's first community orchestra. Small goals, small triumphs—that was all she needed, or wanted. And tonight's triumph, though insignificant by some standards, was the most important of her life . . . which was why Jack

7

would have never considered missing it. Not if he was able to do otherwise.

Forcing the smile to linger on her lips long after the pleasure had begun to fade, Cathy reached for Glen's arm. "We *were* good, weren't we?"

"Better than that," Glen agreed, "we actually sold tickets! We might be the first community orchestra in the history of the world to show a profit in the first year, and if you can do that you don't *have* to be good. But we were good," he added, grinning down at her.

Cathy laughed again. Linking arms, they walked toward the open door, where the night air on the front porch was marginally cooler. Others were there before them, sitting on the steps and the rail, looking like overdressed birds in their concert black and stiff tuxes, flitting from one conversational group to the other and chattering excitedly. Just looking at them, Cathy felt a surge of warmth so intense it almost blotted out the dark shadow of worry that haunted the back of her mind. These were Cathy's closest friends, and tonight they shared a bond that was as strong as family.

Almost.

Elliot Roberts spotted her and raised a glass. "And there she is. The woman of the hour—and perhaps the only musician, male or female, ever to turn down an offer to audition for the Boston Symphony."

"How did you hear about that?" Cathy demanded, but she spotted Ellen, just coming outside, and the expression on her friend's face was entirely too innocent.

To a chorus of, "Are you kidding?" and "Cathy, you didn't!" and "How could you!" Cathy shrugged uncomfortably and tried to grin.

"What can I say? It was an honor just to be asked. Besides, can you see me in that Boston traffic?"

There was some good natured laughter and a few exaggerated groans. "I can't even see you trying to *get* yourself from here to there!" someone joked.

And someone else said, "Not to mention getting back. All things considered, I think we're all a lot better off if you just stay put."

"Besides," Cathy replied brightly, raising her glass, "I might just get the job. And then what would you do without me?"

"And who would take care of Jack and the kids?" Ellen murmured in passing.

Cathy frowned a little, unwilling to admit just how much that consideration had had to do with her refusing the audition — and a little annoyed with Ellen for reading her so easily.

She found an empty spot at the rail and leaned against it, returning the smiles of those who raised their glasses to her, trying to let the good feelings overcome the dread. It had been a triumph, the best night of her life. Why wasn't Jack there to share it?

"You know something?" Glen's voice was casual, and quiet enough to be heard by only her. He looked around the crowd. "You probably could have."

Cathy glanced at him. "Could have what?"

"Gotten that job. You're better than this. Better than all of us."

Cathy made a deprecating noise in her throat, which he ignored.

9

"So how come?" he insisted. It was not the first time he had asked the question. "How did a big fish like you end up in such a little pond?"

"You sound like Jack."

"Jack happens to be right. Not about much, of course, but about this."

He was trying to make her smile again, but this time he didn't succeed. That knot of pain just behind Cathy's forehead started to tighten again, dread and certainty clenching like a fist, and she said softly, "Where *is* he, Glen? What could have happened to him?"

"He's stuck on the highway somewhere," Glen replied promptly, "with a burned-out bearing or a broken timing belt or a thrown rod. You know what kind of care he takes of his car — he thinks it's like a horse, and will keep on running as long as he feeds it."

Cathy shook her head. "He would have called."

"And he will. As soon as he realizes he doesn't have a prayer of fixing it himself and decides to go for help. I know Jack, and I can see him now, standing on the side of the road beating on the engine with a lug wrench."

"Stuck on the highway, with two children . . ." She shuddered elaborately.

"It'll be good for his character."

"I should have gone with them," Cathy worried. "If I was with them —"

"You'd be stuck on the highway, too, and would have missed what will no doubt be the single most memorable cultural event in Lynn Haven history."

Cathy smiled weakly. She wanted to believe Glen

was right. Jack was careless with his cars and was constantly suffering breakdowns. But he was also a mechanical genius, and she could not imagine any problem developing that Jack couldn't fix, any more than she could picture him wasting time trying to make repairs that were beyond his skills. He would know at first glance whether or not he needed professional help, and he wouldn't take any chances with the children in the car. Cathy did not believe mechanical failure had caused the delay. On the other hand, Jack was an excellent driver and had never had an accident in his life. There was no reason for her to think . . .

"It was great, Cathy." Reva Lyons leaned forward to brush her cheek with a kiss. "Concert and party. I wish it could go on forever, but tomorrow's a working day. Happy birthday, kid, and the same to Jack."

"Do you have to go?"

Cathy's dismay was not feigned. Somehow it seemed that as long as the party was going on, as long as people were waiting, there was a chance Jack might still arrive. He might be late, but he wouldn't be absent. But it was eleven o'clock on a Thursday night, and all of the members of the orchestra had day jobs. One by one they began to take their leave, parting with comments like, "We owe it all to you, Cath," and "That Jack doesn't know what he missed," and "Many happy returns, sweetie."

She watched them go with a smile frozen in place and despair sinking to her feet, until at last only Ellen and Glen were left. Glen took her hands, looking at her with concern in his eyes. "Do you want me to stay?"

She shook her head, glancing around the room cluttered with glasses and half-empty bowls and paper plates, and she tried to make her voice bright. "Just send back a cleaning crew, okay?"

His expression was sober. "He's okay, honey. Don't worry."

Swallowing the lump in her throat, Cathy nodded.

He leaned forward and kissed her on the cheek. Then, belying his reassurances, he added, "Call me if you need anything."

Ellen came in from the kitchen, carrying a trash bag in each hand. She waited until Glen was gone to thrust one of the bags toward Cathy and inquire, "You want to tell me again why you're letting him get away?"

Cathy smiled weakly and began to stuff paper plates into the bag. "I don't know. Holding out for a hero, I guess. Jack says . . ." There was a funny little catch in her voice that surprised her, and she had to clear her throat to go on. "Jack says my expectations are too high."

Ellen muttered, bending to empty the remnants of a bowl of popcorn into her bag, "Well, Jack should know, I guess."

Cathy looked at her sharply. "What's that supposed to mean?"

Ellen's expression was immediately apologetic, underscored with guilt. "Look, I'm sorry. I know you're worried about him and I don't mean to criticize. I mean, I know how it is with twins, and after your folks died I guess all you had was each other.

12

But Cathy, you do kind of hero-worship him, you know. I just wonder if . . ."

She let the words trail off, and this time Cathy's smile was tired, but genuine. "If I'm subconsciously measuring every man I meet against the standards set by my twin brother?" She shrugged. "Maybe. Jack has been taking care of me all my life, and there *is* a bond between twins that I can't explain. Of course, it seems like every man I meet wants to take care of me . . ." She gave a self-deprecating shrug. She was a small woman, and her fragile appearance had inspired men's protective instincts throughout her adult life, which was, if she was perfectly honest with herself, a situation Cathy rather enjoyed. "But who needs it on a permanent basis? I like my life the way it is."

Ellen opened her mouth as though to reply to that, but then apparently changed her mind. She busied herself scooping up paper napkins and emptying ashtrays.

Cathy smiled gratefully and reached for the trash bag. "You don't have to stay, you know. I can do this."

Ellen shook her head. "I thought I'd bunk with you tonight, if it's okay. I've had a little too much to drink to be driving . . ." And then she looked at Cathy. "Besides, you don't have to be a twin to know Jack should have called by now. I'll stay."

Once again Cathy had to swallow back the lump in her throat. "You're a good friend," she said huskily.

* * *

The call came at a quarter 'til twelve. Cathy had just showered and changed into her nightshirt, though she had no intention of sleeping, or even trying. Ellen was making up the sofa bed for herself. When the telephone rang Cathy knocked over a lamp in her haste to answer it, and Ellen caught the lamp before it hit the floor.

Her heart was pounding so hard she didn't, at first, understand the voice on the other end. "What?" she demanded hoarsely.

"— Mercy Hospital in Albany, Oregon," the woman's voice repeated. "Is this Cathy Hamilton?"

"Yes." She felt the blood drain from her cheeks. Ellen touched her shoulder.

"Do you have a brother named Jack Hamilton?"

"Yes." Barely a whisper now. "What —"

"Miss Hamilton, I'm afraid there's been an accident. We found your name in his wallet —"

"How bad?" Her voice sounded calm now, amazingly so. Her knuckles were white on the receiver and her arm ached from the pressure, all the way up into her shoulder muscles. "How badly is Jack hurt?"

"His condition is listed as critical, but I'm afraid I don't have any details. He is in surgery now . . ."

She was sitting on the edge of the sofa and she didn't know how she got there. Ellen was gripping her shoulder, her eyes stunned and anxious.

Cathy managed, "The children . . ."

There was a slight pause, just long enough for Cathy to think, *No. Please God, no* . . . Then the woman said, "The children were treated for minor injuries and, pending notification of next of kin, are being kept overnight for observation."

The relief that went through Cathy made her light-headed, and she missed some of the next words. ". . . scheduled for release in the morning. Is there a closer relative we could notify? Otherwise, Family and Children's Services will be granted temporary custody . . ."

"No," Cathy said hoarsely, urgently. "I am. I'm their nearest relative . . ." She tried to take a breath, dragging her hand through her hair, but found it nearly impossible. "I mean, their mother . . . she's in Europe somewhere, no one knows where. They have a maternal grandmother in Cincinnati. I don't — I can't remember her number — but it doesn't matter, she's too far away. I'll be there before morning. I'm leaving now."

"Excuse me, but if you could give us the number of the grandmother . . ."

"I told you, I don't — "

But Ellen was thrusting an address book in front of Cathy. She stared at it blankly for an endless moment, then began to thumb the pages with shaking fingers. Of course the hospital needed to know. She was the children's grandmother — someone had to call her.

Cathy found the address, which she had never expected to use for anything other than Christmas cards, and beside it the phone number. She read the information aloud. "But I'm leaving now," she repeated to the voice on the other end of the phone. "I'll be there. Tell Jack . . . I'll be there."

She didn't know what else was said, if anything. She didn't even remember hanging up the phone,

15

going to her bedroom, pulling on her jeans, snatching up her purse.

Ellen said, "Let me go with you. It's the middle of the night, you shouldn't go alone . . ."

Cathy shook her head frantically. "I don't know how long I'll be. I don't know what—" She had to draw a deep breath then, literally gasping it in like a diver surfacing for air. "He was in surgery. I don't know how serious. The kids . . . I have to get there. The kids . . ."

Janie and Christopher, age five, all alone in a strange hospital room, their daddy hurt and their Aunt Cathy so far away . . . how terrified they must be. How lost and alone. Cathy tried not to think about it. She couldn't think about it, she couldn't start crying, not now. She had to get there. She had to get to Jack, she had to be there for his children.

Ellen thrust an overnight bag into her hands and Cathy stared at it for a moment as though she had never seen it before. Had she packed it, or had Ellen?

"Maps," Ellen said. "Do you have maps?"

Cathy pushed past her. "I'll ask directions."

"What about money?"

"I think so."

Ellen followed her to the porch. "For God's sake Cathy, are you okay to drive?"

Cathy nodded distractedly, then turned to hug her friend briefly, fiercely. "Stay here tonight, will you, in case they try to call?"

Ellen squeezed her hands tightly. "Of course I will. You call me the minute you get there. No, call me sooner, from the road, in case . . ."

Cathy nodded, turning for the steps.

Ellen caught her arm. "Cathy, for God's sake be careful!"

"I will," she answered, or thought she answered; she didn't really know. She tossed her bag and her purse into the car and climbed in, slamming the door behind her.

Ellen's face was at the open window. "Cathy . . ."

But her eyes were full of helplessness and she didn't know what to say, and that was when Cathy felt the tears burn her throat. She had to look away.

"I'll call," she promised hoarsely, and she started the engine.

Ellen stood in the driveway until she was out of sight, but Cathy didn't look back.

Chapter Two

Cathy's hands tightened on the steering wheel as she guided the car, looking for the service station that belonged to the Amoco sign she'd seen from the expressway. So far she'd passed a Gulf station and a Texaco, both closed, and she'd gone at least a mile out of her way. What if the Amoco was closed too?

At one-thirty in the morning the only people on the streets in Portersville, California were looking for trouble. Decent people had long since closed their curtains and set their alarm clocks. Stores and roadside marts had closed; neon signs were dark, shutters were down. Streetlights were few and far between. There were no bars, nightclubs, or late-night movies, and restaurants had turned off the lights on their marquees. Along the narrow access road that ran above the expressway, Cathy Hamilton's car was the only thing that moved.

A catch of panic, dry and stale, dug into the back of her throat, and Cathy swallowed it back quickly. The fuel indicator read a quarter of a tank, and in the Honda that could mean another hundred miles or so. She would go farther up the expressway if she had to; but she didn't want to. For the past fifteen minutes the need to call the hospital had been pressing down on her, and she didn't think she could wait any longer. She had been driving an hour and she didn't know how much farther it was to Albany, Oregon . . . six hours? Eight? Three? How could she go even three more hours without knowing . . . something?

A new panic caught her unexpectedly, roiling up in her chest like a dust storm of smothering proportions. *Jack, don't die. God, don't die, please* . . .

She saw the Amoco station.

The sign that towered over the surrounding landscape and could be seen for half a mile in either direction from the expressway belonged to a minimart with two self-service pumps and a faded "Open Twenty-Four Hours" sign in the window. About twenty yards away from the building was a telephone stand.

As she swung into the parking lot Cathy saw the first signs of life since leaving the expressway. One car was just pulling away from the pumps. Two others were parked in the shadows, and one of them was empty. A dark blue sedan was pulled close to a dumpster at the side of the building, and two men in the front seat looked as though they were waiting for someone. The man in the driver's seat was wearing a faded red fishing cap and a plaid shirt, the passenger was drinking a styrofoam cup of coffee. Inside the brightly lit store she could see a teenage clerk and a male customer.

Cathy registered all this with a part of her mind

19

that was always actively recording details without really stopping to notice them at all, nor caring what those details meant. Jack sometimes teased her about her inability to see the forest for the trees. In the orchestra she became so absorbed in the sounds of each individual instrument that she rarely heard the symphony; she compulsively alphabetized her spices and arranged her closet according to color, but could let the dishes pile up for days without noticing, and rarely made her bed. It was a form of tunnel vision, and she lived her life the same way: it was a series of details, each unconnected to the others but somehow forming a larger picture that, more often than not, escaped her.

She pulled close to the telephone stand and fumbled in her purse for her credit card. A black man in a denim jacket came out of the store as she reached the telephone. It was twenty minutes before two.

She had to spend some time in the dim light of the telephone trying to decipher the directions for use of the card. She never made long distance calls away from home. She didn't even know why she carried a telephone card. She never traveled, she didn't like to leave home, she had no one to call but Jack . . .

Finally she dialed the operator. "I want to make a credit card call to Mercy Hospital in Albany, Oregon. I don't know the number."

"The number for long distance information is—"

"No! I don't want information. This is an emergency."

"May I have your credit card number, please?"

Cathy gave her number and waited for the sequence of electronic bleeps and switches for the call to be completed. She caught a fuzzy glimpse of her reflection in the three-sided plexiglass that surrounded the phone booth: a white face surrounded by an unkempt mass of dark hair, punctuated by eyes that were too big and too shocked-looking to be her own. The blue nightshirt with its honey-bear transfer on the front was half tucked into and half trailing out of her jeans. *I should have at least brushed my hair,* she thought, focusing once again on details to keep her mind off the beating of her heart, which grew louder and more insistent with each breath. *I'll have to put on makeup before I see Jack. Maybe I have some blush in my purse . . .*

"I'm sorry, that line is busy."

"Busy?" Cathy's hand, braced against the body of the telephone, tightened on the slick plastic. "How can it be busy? It's a hospital, it's one-thirty in the morning — "

"I'm sorry," the operator repeated firmly. "Please try your call again in a few minutes."

Cathy pressed the disconnect hook and took another few deep breaths. Busy. A small-town hospital, probably only one operator on duty, that was okay. She'd try again. First she would get gas, then she'd call Ellen, just in case, then she would try the hospital again.

She started to replace the receiver, and then she noticed, superimposed upon her own reflection, the black man coming toward her. Some instinct warned her to stay where she was, with her hand on the disconnect and the receiver braced against her shoulder, pretending to ignore him as she watched his reflection come closer. It would be much harder to snatch a purse here in this small enclosure than out in the open, and if she didn't meet his eyes maybe he would walk on by. Maybe he just wanted to use the telephone.

She felt the muscles around her skull go tense, and she held her breath as his shadow fell over her, blotting out his reflection. He moved with an easy, casual gait, hands in pockets, head slightly bent, looking neither right nor left. Cathy's fingers dug into the receiver.

The man passed close by her but didn't stop. He said in a low voice, without looking at her, "It's off tonight, babe. You've been made."

And he continued walking straight past her, toward a red Corvette parked near the curb.

The skin on the back of Cathy's neck crawled. She didn't move, she didn't stare, she barely breathed. She had, in fact, no time to react at all, or even to register what she had heard, because the telephone suddenly shrilled in her ear.

She jumped, and her hand automatically released the disconnect hook. A voice, husky and male, said, "Nine oh double-u one five, four oh en oh two."

A coldness gripped Cathy's spine; her heart was thundering wildly. Details, none of which made sense. Three cars parked at an out-of-the-way mini-mart in an otherwise deserted town. A cryptic warning from a black man. A call that was not meant for her. Two men in a blue sedan watching her. It didn't have to make sense. Something was very wrong here.

Christ, she thought. She replaced the receiver and took a step back from the telephone stand. Behind

her, she heard a car door open. She looked frantically toward her own car, which suddenly seemed
too far away. *Christ . . .*

In the blue sedan Dave Jenks and Toby Miller
watched alertly and tried to pretend that the adrenaline surge was nothing more than too much caf-
feine. They spent six nights out of ten like this,
following leads they never expected to pan out, and
there was no reason to think this night would be any
different.

They had spent the last three hours drinking coffee, eating stale chips out of a bag, and playing one
of those word games Toby was all the time pulling
out of his hat; this one was naming a word that
ended in the first letter of the last word named.
Dave groused about the games and Toby kept making them up just to irritate him, but Dave always
played along. There was a part of him that enjoyed
the challenge even when he was over his head, as he
often was with Toby.

Toby was fifteen years younger than Dave and
lacked that much experience, but it rarely, if ever,
showed. Dave had resented that unexpected competence on the part of the younger man at first, but
over the three years they had been partners he had
had more than one occasion to be grateful for it.
Toby could be a smart-ass at times, but he was a
good-natured one, and he knew when to admit he
was wrong. He was going to college part-time and
said he wanted to be a lawyer, but Dave tried not to
hold that against him. Dave was neither very intel-

lectual nor ambitious, but he had a secret admiration for those who were. Besides, if he thought back far enough Dave, too, could remember a time when he had wanted to be something other than an aging cop in a fading town.

"Xenophobia," said Toby, just as the woman in the red Honda pulled up.

"What the hell is that?" Dave watched the woman get out of the car and start toward the telephone.

"Somebody who's afraid of what they don't understand. Different races, cultures, that kind of thing." They were both watching the woman now.

"Shit. Your head is just full of that crap, isn't it? Who the hell ever uses a word like that?"

Toby said, "She's ten minutes late."

Dave grunted.

"Doesn't look much like I expected."

Dave drained the dregs of his lukewarm coffee and crumpled the cup on the dashboard. The woman at the telephone was small-figured, with shoulder-length curly black hair that could have benefited from the use of a comb. Her skin was so fair that in the parking lot lights it looked almost fluorescent. The jeans and big tee shirt she wore looked a little rumpled, and she carried an oversize canvas purse that somehow didn't go with the image he had formed of her. He supposed he, too, had expected someone a bit more exotic.

He shrugged and said, "They never do."

Out of the corner of his eye Dave saw the black man leave the store and start toward her. Toby saw it too and put his hand on the door handle.

"Wait," Dave said. "See what happens."

24

Toby muttered, "Geez, I hate coming into the middle of a game where I don't know the players."

They both settled back tensely to watch.

The black man passed by her. He may have spoken to her, but they were too far away to hear and she gave no sign. Toby risked glancing at Dave. He said uneasily, "You know, I'm starting not to like this."

"You're just xenophobic." But Dave knew the feeling. Suddenly, what had started out to be a routine operation seemed a little too pat, and at the same time shot full of holes. Or maybe he had spent too many nights waiting for nothing to happen. Maybe he just got spooked when something actually did.

"It could be a setup."

"Or she could just be calling her babysitter."

But the guy in the denim jacket hadn't walked fifteen feet out of his way just to smell her perfume. It had looked like a contact to Dave. To both of them.

"I still don't see why we didn't just take the call ourselves."

"She's being watched. We move toward the phone and there's no call."

It followed that they, too, were under surveillance, and waiting didn't make their position any safer. But they were both trying not to think about that now. They really hadn't expected it to go this far.

Dave added, "We wait 'til she takes the call, then move in on her. Carefully."

"If there is a call."

Dave said, "Is that with an x or a z?"

"Figure it out yourself."

The phone rang.

Dave murmured, "Well, what d'ya know about that? Looks like we hit pay dirt." His heart was beating hard.

"So now it gets fun. Who's the lucky man?"

"I vote for the guy that knows how to spell xenophobia."

Toby opened the door and Dave picked up the radio mike. "Suspect appears to have made contact," he said. "We're moving in."

Cathy had pulled the car against the curb sloppily, so that she had to walk all the way around the back to get to the driver's door. Her heart was beating so rapidly that everything else, even the movement of her legs, seemed in slow motion. She tried to get her keys out of her purse. Hadn't Jack told her a dozen times never to wait until she got to her car to look for her keys? Those few moments, standing in the dark, fumbling in her purse for her keys, were when a woman was most vulnerable to attack. She was in the dark now, and she could hear footsteps coming up behind her; the lighted mini-mart was less than fifty yards away but it might as well have been across a chasm. The footsteps were getting closer and she had never felt more vulnerable in her life.

The hand closed around her upper arm just as she reached for the door, and her knees went weak. She remembered all the things Jack had tried to teach her about kicking and gouging and screaming at the

26

top of her lungs; in her line of work she was out a lot late at night and he worried about her safety. In a town like Lynn Haven there wasn't much to worry about, but Cathy had always thought she could take care of herself. She had always imagined her reflexes quick, her outrage empowering, her survival instinct sharp. But the stranger gripped her arm hard enough to shoot bolts of pain through her shoulder, a wave of terror choked off her breath, and she gasped, "Oh, please, let me go . . . don't hurt me . . ."

"Stay cool and nobody is going to get hurt." His voice was low and controlled. The pressure on her arm dragged her a few steps forward. "We're going to walk very quietly over to that car and have us a little talk."

Another bolt of sharp-edged terror stabbed at her as she glanced frantically toward the car, where the man in the red cap was waiting. She looked desperately up at her captor and registered a blurred impression of a man younger than she was, with red hair and fair skin that was sprinkled with freckles, and she thought, *Do something! Run, scream, fight* . . . But he was stronger than she was—his grip was unbreakable. The self-loathing that rose up inside her was almost as paralyzing as the fear as she pleaded, "Please, I'll do anything you say, just let me—"

She did not recognize the loud cracking sound that split the night, nor did she register the significance of the droplets of moisture that splattered her skin and the front of her nightshirt. She only knew that the grip on her arm was suddenly released; the red-haired man was thrown away from her so abruptly that she staggered and almost fell, and she was free.

She tore at the door-handle of her car, which mercifully she had forgotten to lock after all, and flung herself inside. There was a shout and another sharp crack, and that was when Cathy noticed the black man in the denim jacket stagger and fall not five feet away from her, close enough that she could see the shock on his face and hear his gun scrape against the asphalt as it flew from his fingers. Details, played out against the background of her mind like a television show she watched with only half her attention. Meanwhile, her fingers scrambled through her purse and a greater part of her mind was screaming, *Keys . . . keys . . . dear God, let me find them . . .*

In the distance was the sound of sobs, which might have been her own. Outside, muffled by the glass of her closed window, more shouts. The key ring was in her hand but the key would not fit in the ignition. She cried out in frustration and her heart missed a beat as she fumbled with the keys and almost dropped them on the floor. She could hear running footsteps. *Oh, God, please . . .*

The second key fit the ignition and she turned it violently. The starter screamed in protest and she slammed the gearshift into drive. As she turned the wheel hard to the right, her front tires bounced off the curb, and there, for a moment, she had a glimpse of two bodies on the pavement. Bodies. Dead men. Someone had a gun and two people were dead. *Dead . . .*

She pressed down on the accelerator and the car

swung around wildly, almost out of control, slamming up and over the apron that circled the mini-mart. The man in the red cap was running toward her, his face grim, with a gun steadied in both hands and leveled straight at her. She pushed the accelerator to the floor and the tires screamed, the passenger door scraped against the side of the building with a whine of metal on brick, and the car shot out into the street.

She did not notice another car slide out of the shadows on the opposite side of the street, headlights off, and begin to follow her.

Chapter Three

The town of Portersville, California was like dozens of others along the interstate — not too big, not too prosperous, built around retirement villages and the occasional tourist who was lured off the interstate by signs promising fresh produce, gas, and souvenirs. There were better motels up the road, and better restaurants, and more interesting scenery. No one stopped for long in Portersville, and it was basically a quiet town.

The average wage was $4.75 an hour. The biggest law-enforcement problem, in terms of frequency, was burglary. Portersville had its share of drug traffic, but no more than any other town its size, and the police department was satisfied that the problem was kept pretty much under control. When there was a murder in Portersville it made the headlines for weeks. No one was prepared for random slaughter, and no officer had been killed in the line of duty for over five years.

Three minutes after Dave had clutched the radio microphone in his hands and shouted, "Officer down! Officer down!" two cruisers swung into the parking lot with sirens blaring and dome lights swinging wild blue circles through the night. Thirty seconds after that, three more units pulled up, and in the distance Dave could hear the baleful in-and-out wail of an ambulance. He was holding Toby's head on his knees and he knew the ambulance would arrive too late.

The bullet's entry had shattered Toby's spine, which was a mercy. The exit wound was a baseball-sized hole that pumped blood in rhythmic fountains through the ragged edges of Toby's shirt, just above his belt. No amount of pressure would stop the bleeding. The pavement was slick with it.

Toby's breathing was irregular and wet with blood bubbles. Dave wondered how he could have stayed alive this long, with blood gushing out of his stomach by the pint and bits of charred flesh splattered all over his clothing. He was glad Toby couldn't feel the pain. He wanted to say something, something encouraging, something meaningful, something a man could say to somebody who'd been his partner and his best friend for three years and taken his ribbing and overlooked his foul moods and always been ready to go through the door first. Dave was thinking a lot of things: how he'd never told Toby it was good to have him around, or that he was a fine cop; how it should have been Toby who stayed behind with the radio instead of Dave; how he should have seen it coming, acted quicker; how he was going to miss Toby's intellectual bullshit and dry wit . . . But somehow those thoughts never made it into words, and he couldn't have said them anyway.

There was a knot in his throat that burned and stabbed, and he wasn't sure whether it was from rage or pain. But he could hardly get a breath around it, much less words, so he just held Toby's head and watched him bleed and willed him to hold on a few minutes longer, though he knew it would do no good.

The ambulance swung into the parking lot. The noise was deafening. Cops were everywhere, but Dave didn't hear them, barely saw them. Toby was looking at him, his eyes unfocused and fogged over and not like Toby at all. He whispered, "It was an *x*." And he died.

Dave stood up slowly. The knees of his pants were soggy with blood that had pooled on the pavement. Two paramedics bent over Toby. A gurney rattled over the asphalt. Dave turned away.

Police Chief Sam Hayforth stood in front of him, his head down, his hands stuffed deep into the pockets of his J C Penney slacks. He demanded quietly, "What happened?"

The knot in Dave's throat dissolved into bile and seemed to release a dam of rage and impotence inside him. He looked at the other man, with his balding head and his lightweight cotton jacket, and he wanted to spit. He wanted to hit something.

"You tell me," he answered quietly, with deliberate control. He was shaking inside. "You sent us out here to pick up an informant. One-thirty, you said. She's ready to cooperate. Wait for the phone call. Be careful, she might spook. We were here. We waited. We were careful. Now you tell me. *What* ~~the fuck~~ *went wrong?*"

Hayforth raised his eyes to Dave's and held his gaze, calm and steady. The intent was not to shame Dave, nor to intimidate him, but simply to remind him of who and where he was. After a long time, it worked.

Dave felt the wild animal inside him recede and settle into the shadows, controlled if not subdued. The flaring rage was replaced by a thick ache in his throat that spread all the way down to his chest. He glanced briefly toward Toby, who was being lifted onto the gurney. He looked away before the sheet was drawn up to cover his face.

He said stiffly, "By one-thirty, we thought she wasn't going to show. There was the usual amount of traffic in and out of here. It was hard to spot anything suspicious. She pulled in about twenty 'til two. Went straight to the phone. That guy over there . . ." he nodded toward the black man sprawled on the pavement, "went up to her, might've said something. We didn't interfere. Maybe he warned her, I don't know. She got the phone call. Toby went to take her in. She looked like she'd changed her mind. Scared. She tried to get away. Before I knew what was happening . . ." He swallowed hard. "The black dude opened fire. Maybe he was aiming for her, maybe it was Toby. I nailed him, but by that time she was in her car, burning rubber."

Hayforth said, "It wasn't your fault."

Maybe that was true, but it didn't make Dave feel any better.

Dave said softly, "I want that woman. My partner's dead and she's the reason why."

The chief nodded. "We'll put an APB on the

car. She won't get far."

Hayforth walked over to the body of the black man. Dave followed him. A second ambulance had arrived but the paramedics were standing by uselessly, waiting for the forensics team that was being called in from the next town. On the concrete apron of the building, a uniformed officer was interviewing the teenage clerk, whose acne-scarred face gleamed white and terrified in the wash of the store lights.

Dave stared down at the body. He said flatly, not really expecting an answer, "Who was he?"

"His name was Deke Clemmons." From nowhere, a man in a windbreaker and khaki pants stood at their sides. "He worked for a man called Delcastle."

He pulled out an ID folder and passed it to Hayforth. "Scott Kreiger," he said, "DEA. You can cancel that all-points. I'm taking over here."

Cathy had driven perhaps three miles before she realized her headlights were off. Street signs, driveways, and billboards flashed by in a blur of gray and white; the asphalt whined beneath her wheels, her breath made ragged hissing sounds on its way out of her throat. The road curved sharply and a utility pole suddenly sprang in front of her. She cut the wheel to the left and the back tires skidded on the opposite shoulder before the car straightened out again. She reached forward and turned the headlights switch with shaking fingers.

She didn't know where she was going. She didn't know where she was. She couldn't think back; she couldn't bring up a picture of two men sprawled on the pavement and the sound of gunfire ringing in her ears, or she'd start screaming. She had to drive, just *drive,* she had to get away . . .

The world was filled with muggers, rapists, psychotic killers, and child abusers. Cathy saw them every night on the news: elderly people savagely beaten to death by teenagers who were just out for fun, men who settled imaginary injustices by walking into a mall and firing an assault rifle into the crowd, drug kingpins who waged virtual war on small towns. She saw these things, recoiled from them in mild repulsion, and closed her curtains and went on about her business, because horrors like that had nothing to do with her life.

Bad things didn't happen to Cathy Hamilton. She knew small troubles and minor challenges and the everyday victories that went along with them. The car that wouldn't start, the credit card payment that got lost in the mail, the TV picture tube that went out three days after the warranty expired. Her world was uncomplicated and predictable, and she kept it that way almost by force of will; she simply could not tolerate any deviation from the norm. People did not call in the middle of the night to say that her brother had been in an accident. People didn't threaten her with guns or try to force her into strange cars or send her fleeing for her life down a strange highway in the middle of nowhere.

But the man in the red hat had pointed a gun at her. He had wanted to kill her. Two men were dead. She'd seen it with her own eyes. She hadn't wanted to, she hadn't meant to, but it had happened . . .

Oh Jack, oh God, don't let this be happening . . .

Her cheeks were wet with tears, and her whole body was shaking so badly it was hard to keep the car under control. She glanced at the speedometer and saw she was doing over sixty on the narrow, unfamiliar road. She eased off the accelerator, but not much. Pushing her hand over her face, she tried to clear her eyes, and managed an almost steady breath. She glanced at the passing landscape and all of it looked the same. She had missed the expressway. She didn't know where she was. She couldn't think, she didn't know what to do . . .

Jack would have known what to do. He was always ready to cope, never out of his depth. He was connected to reality in a way she was not nor ever would be; he had always kept her feet on the ground. He was the part of her that was rational and organized, the voice of reason when things started to fly apart; he always knew what to do.

Stop. He would have said. *Calm down. Take a deep breath. Think.*

She tried to draw in a breath. It got choked in her throat. She tried again.

Her brother was lying in a hospital hundreds of miles away, his children were depending on her, and all she wanted to do was get to them. They were all the family she had left and they needed her, they were all that mattered. If she tried hard enough she could pretend she had never stopped at that mini-mart and everything that had come afterwards had never happened. She could keep driving, and she wouldn't have to deal with this.

But she *had* to deal with it. Someone had tried to

kidnap her. Another man had tried to shoot her. Now two people were dead and she didn't know why. She had to call the police. Jack would have insisted that she call the police. It was the only sane thing to do.

But she didn't want to stop the car, she didn't want to walk up to another deserted phone booth and try to make another call, as though the mere act of doing so would be tempting fate. In the car was safety, protection, purpose. Every minute she delayed was another minute apart from Jack, and Jack needed her, Jack was the only thing that mattered . . .

She could almost see his dark scowl. *Escapism again, Cathy. This is not going to go away just because you ignore it. You've got to deal with this.*

"Yes, I know," she whispered. She brought an unsteady hand to her face again, pushing back her hair. "I will. I'll deal with it." But it would require more courage than she thought she possessed to get out of the car again, and all she could think of was getting to Jack, just driving until the miles piled up between herself and the nightmare at the mini-mart and she was somehow safe again.

The interior of the car was lit abruptly by a brilliant light. The suddenness of it made her gasp and shield her eyes, momentarily disoriented. She looked in the rearview mirror and the glare of headlights, directly behind her and too close for safety, stabbed at her eyes. The car had come from nowhere and was now riding her bumper, lights on high beam.

She glanced at the speedometer. Fifty miles an

hour. The car remained just inches off her bumper, and the bright lights made her eyes ache. She didn't need this now. God, she couldn't deal with this . . .

She lifted her foot off the accelerator, slowing so that the car could pass. The speedometer dropped to forty-five, forty. The light that flooded her car didn't diminish. She tapped the brakes. The car behind her slowed accordingly but didn't leave her bumper. Her heart tightened in her throat.

Her first instinct was to pull over, stop, and let him go around. She might even try to flag him down and ask for help. And she could almost hear Jack's voice saying, *Don't be a fool. After what happened, out here in the middle of nowhere . . . Cathy,* think, *for God's sake.*

Cautiously, she pressed down on the accelerator. The car behind her kept pace. "Oh, God," she whispered.

He wasn't following her. She was sure of that. Just a late night traveler in a hurry, maybe drunk — maybe he'd spotted a lone woman on the road and thought he'd have a little fun. In a minute he'd go around. He *had* to go around, because Cathy couldn't take this now, she couldn't allow herself to believe that anything else bad could happen. The nightmare had to end.

The road on which she was traveling was a two-lane state highway, flanked on either side by shallow ditches that occasionally gave way to gently sloping embankments. It was flat and mostly straight, and there was nothing — not a house, not a billboard, not a traffic sign — on either side as far as she could see. Patches of brush and scrub grass flashed by, surreally illuminated by the headlights of the car behind her. Her heart was pounding against the wall of her chest. Her hands were sweaty on the steering wheel. What was that maniac trying to do? Why didn't he go around?

The sound of a horn blared in her ears. Startled, she lost acceleration. The horn went on and on, one long, loud demanding blast, and suddenly it changed direction. The headlights flashed away from her mirror. He was coming around.

She caught a glimpse of the car: long and neutral-colored, light- or mid-green, with a single male driver. He pulled in front of her and speeded up, taillights swaying crazily.

The breath of relief that left Cathy's lungs made her chest ache. A gush of perspiration soaked her armpits, and she felt dizzy. But before her hands could even relax on the steering wheel there was a squeal of brakes and a flash of lights, and the car in front of her suddenly pulled across the road, blocking both lanes, and stopped.

He was less than fifty yards in front of her, and those fifty yards spun out beneath the wheels of Cathy's car in slow motion. A series of details, detached flashes of truth, seconds counting down to certain death. He wanted her to stop. He was trying to force her off the road. She couldn't stop. There was no time. She was going to crash into that car and they both would die. Shock and confusion had caused her foot to stab the accelerator instead of the brake pedal, and the speedometer quivered at sixty and there was no time to pull back, she couldn't react fast enough. Wind and road noise hummed at her window. Ribbons of asphalt shoulder flashed by on either side and the hood of the gray car rushed closer, its headlights washing over a thick embankment of wild shrubs, its taillights glowing off a heavy utility pole. Trapped. She was trapped.

She could see the driver's profile, momentarily caught in the beam of her lights. He was calm, unconcerned, waiting. She couldn't stop. The gray fender loomed in front of her. She cut the wheel and braced for impact.

Cathy screamed as the Honda plowed into the embankment. Branches crashed against the windshield and the car tilted to the right, throwing her sideways in her seat and almost wrenching the steering wheel from her hand. She fought for control as the tires whined for traction and bounced off dirt and gravel and suddenly, unexpectedly, leapt off the embankment and seized the road again.

Cathy's shoulders sagged and she sobbed dryly. But she did not slow down. And she did not look back.

Three miles later there was a warning sign, announcing an upcoming traffic light. Some part of her mind registered it, some part of her mind was still able to think, but the thoughts seemed detached from her, without emotion or reaction or even much significance. The light was red, and Cathy did not even slow down. She remembered a crime show Jack and she had watched once. "A fleeing suspect always takes the first right turn," he had observed. "It's instinct. That's how the cops always find them." Cathy swung the car wildly to the left. The back tires screamed and the front tires bounced off the opposite curb, but she barely noticed. The car straightened out again.

Vaguely she registered the signs of civilization as they spun by her window: a bank, a church, a deserted McDonald's. Street lights. Safety. She began to slow down. Then she could hear the sound of her own breathing, wet and ragged and punctuated with hiccoughing sobs, echoing above the hum of the engine.

On the left was a shopping center with a Kroger, a Hallmark store, a small drugstore. Across the street was a low brick elementary school. She swung sharply into the Kroger parking lot. There was a telephone booth in front of the supermarket.

She stopped the car and spent a moment with her arms crossed over the steering wheel and her head resting against them, shaking uncontrollably. *Over,* she kept trying to tell herself. *It's over.*

But it wasn't over. The taste of what had happened back there on the highway would stay with her the rest of her life.

She straightened up; she opened her purse with jerky, convulsive movements. She found a quarter but couldn't hold on to it; she dropped it three times before closing her palm around it.

She opened the car door and, in the courtesy lights, noticed for the first time the blotchy brown stains on her arms and the front of her jeans. At first she didn't understand the significance, but suddenly it was horrifyingly clear. Blood. A dead man's blood had splashed all over her.

A cry rose up in her throat but was choked back by nausea. She tried to scrub away the stains with her nightshirt but realized that it, too, was splattered with blood. She pushed herself out of the car and stumbled to the telephone booth.

She inserted the quarter and dialed 911 with fingers so shaky they could hardly complete the movements. When a voice answered, "Emergency," she went weak and sagged against the booth for support.

"Please," she whispered brokenly, "you've got to help me . . ."

Chapter Four

In his fifteen years on the force, Dave Jenks had never met a DEA man, but he held a stereotypical picture of one in his head: long hair, scruffy beard, frayed jeans, and bloodshot eyes. In his fifteen years, Dave had never shot to kill before, either. This was a night for firsts.

Scott Kreiger was so far to the right of Dave's preconceived image that it was almost comical. His hair was blond and neatly trimmed around the ears, thinning on top. He had a sallow, lupine face, and pale blue eyes that seemed to sink into the rest of his features so that they were hardly noticeable. Dave didn't trust a man whose eyes he couldn't read.

Kreiger had a quiet, slow way of moving, and a cool voice with the trace of an Ivy League accent. He was put together well enough to stand in a high-priced department store window, and even his name sounded like it belonged to an investment broker. After twenty minutes in his company, the mild suspicion Dave felt had turned into an active dislike.

"I want her whereabouts reported as soon as your men trace her," Kreiger was saying. "But I don't want her apprehended or interfered with in any way. Just keep her in sight. Is that understood?"

They were in the chief's office—or what served as an office in the small, utilitarian police station. The enclosure was little more than a plywood-and-glass partition in the center of the room, and clacking typewriters, ringing phones, and voices carried clearly from the other side. However, it had a door that closed and gave the illusion of privacy. Chief Hayforth had invited Kreiger back to the station to discuss the details of the case; Dave supposed it showed some measure of interagency cooperation that Kreiger had agreed. But he didn't sound as though he was cooperating; he sounded like he was giving orders.

That Hayforth noticed this fact, and resented it as much as Dave, was evident in his expression as he said, "We don't have the manpower to mount that kind of undercover operation, Mr. Kreiger."

"You don't have to. Just keep your black and whites moving. I'll do the rest."

Dave wanted to know why he wasn't doing something now. He wanted to know why they all weren't doing something. He wanted to know what a DEA man was doing in Portersville, California, and why he was working alone, and why he had stood by and let a young cop get shot through the spine for the sake of a phone call. He wanted to know a lot of things.

But what he said was, "Who is she?"

His voice had a flat, dull sound to it, as though he was bored, or very tired. He was neither. He guessed he was in some kind of shock, but he didn't feel that either. What he felt was a low and powerful rage that surged and receded in waves. The effort it took to keep those waves under control used all the energy he had to spare.

Kreiger glanced at him. He seemed to consider whether or not the question was worth the time it took to answer, then replied, "We think her name is Laura. She's Delcastle's girlfriend, one of the best-kept secrets of the underworld. He guards her like the crown jewels. Now maybe you'd like to tell me what you boys know about her."

Hayforth answered that one. "We had a call from an anonymous female yesterday morning. Said she had some information on a drug deal, and the details were coming through from a phone call at the booth on Ray Street at one-thirty. We were to pick her up there."

"So, she was ready to turn." Kreiger wrinkled his forehead a little, as though he had smelled something unpleasant. "Dangerous business."

Dave felt the wave rising again. He pushed it back. He tried to make his voice sound as offhand as Kreiger's, and didn't quite succeed. "How come heavyweights like Delcastle and the DEA are interested in a penny-ante drug bust in a town like this?"

Again Kreiger fixed him with that faded, disinterested stare. "You call thirty-three million in import penny-ante?"

Hayforth straightened a little in his chair. "What the hell are you talking about?"

Kreiger smiled thinly. "Looks like you boys stumbled into something a little over your heads. Not much goes on in a little town like Portersville, right? No need to keep an eye out for anything unusual. So what better place to kick off one of the biggest deals of the year?" He shrugged. "He would have made it, too, if the girl hadn't gotten nervous. Sometimes you just can't figure on the unexpected."

Hayforth said tightly, "Are you telling me that you expect a thirty-three million dollar deal to go down in my town?"

"Unlikely." Kreiger's voice was negligent, almost dismissive. "My feeling is this was just an information relay. The actual transaction will probably take place somewhere more convenient."

"Where?"

"If I knew that, I wouldn't be wasting time here, now would I?"

Dave listened with only part of his mind, not making much sense of the words and not really caring. He had changed his bloodstained trousers for clean ones, but he kept wiping his palms on the knees, as though he could still feel the dampness soaking through to his skin. It sometimes seemed as though if he closed his eyes and opened them again he would still be sitting in that parked car outside the mini-mart, drinking coffee and playing a stupid word game. At other times it seemed like a decade had passed since then, and it was hard to remember what the previous hour had been like.

He said, "You knew what was going down. You knew about the woman. Why wasn't that place swarming with DEA men? Why did you let my partner walk into a trap? Why did you wait until two men were dead to step up and introduce yourself? Can you tell me that?"

Dave was aware of a sharp look from the chief, but Kreiger's expression was impassive. He said, "I didn't know about the woman. Nobody did. I was following Clemmons, but lost him. I didn't even get there until too late."

Dave grinned feebly. There was no mirth behind the expression, but it felt good to try. "Hell of a mess, huh, Kreiger? And you've got the balls to walk in here and tell us you're taking over."

He got to his feet abruptly. "I'm going to see if DMV has got anything on that car yet."

Kreiger said sharply, "I didn't order a trace."

"Looks like there's a lot of things you didn't do."

Hayforth stood. "Let it go, Dave. This isn't your case anymore."

Dave opened the door.

Kreiger took a step forward. He said quietly, "Maybe I didn't make myself clear."

"You made yourself clear enough." Dave turned on him. The wave swelled and crested, and he couldn't hold it back. "You made it clear that a good man is dead and you're not interested in that. The only person who can tell us why is roaming around out there free, and you're not interested in that either. You've lost your suspect and your chance to bust a thirty-three million dollar deal, and what you've made clear, Mr. Kreiger, is that you've ▓▓▓▓▓ up and you don't know what to do now. So if you'll just stay out of my way—"

"Dave!"

It was Anne, the dispatcher, and her voice, sharp with urgency, cut through the red haze of Dave's fury. She said, "Pick up on the emergency line. It's a woman who says she was at the shooting."

Dave rushed toward the nearest phone. Kreiger followed, and Dave thought he was going to try to stop him, but all he said was, "Just listen. Let your dispatcher do the talking."

Dave wanted to argue, but for once the other man made sense. The woman was spooked already, and there was no point complicating matters.

He said to Anne, "Find out where she is," and picked up a phone. Kreiger pushed a detective aside to get to another phone, and Hayforth listened in his office.

There was no mistaking the terror in the woman's voice. She said, "Please, I don't know what to do. Someone is following me, a man, I think he wants to kill me—"

Dave looked sharply at Kreiger, who didn't

return the glance.

Anne said, "Can you tell me where you are?"

"I don't know! I'm not from around here, I—" There was a catching sound, like a sob, and a pause with only the sound of her breathing.

Anne looked at Dave. She said, "Look around. What do you see?"

"I'm in—in a phone booth. There's a Kroger and—and a shoe shop, and a Rosefield Pharmacy—"

Dave signaled affirmation to Anne. Anne said, "What is your name?"

"Please, I'm so scared—"

Dave replaced his receiver. "I'm on my way."

Anne said, "Listen to me. Stay right where you are. We're sending a car for you."

Dave checked his weapon on the way to the door. Hayforth's voice didn't stop him. Kreiger stepped out in front of him. "Back to your desk, detective. I'll handle this."

Dave looked over his shoulder at Hayforth. "Are you going to send a black and white, or am I going alone?"

There was just enough hesitation to let Dave know that Hayforth was on his side. "You've got a report to make out."

"I told you, you people are off this case. I'm not having any interference from the locals."

Dave looked at Kreiger. "I couldn't give a shit about your case. I'm a police officer answering a 911 from a woman in distress, and I want to see you try to stop me."

49

"I can."

"And while you're trying, your famous Laura—and your drug bust—slip through your fingers. Get out of my way." He pushed toward the door.

Kreiger caught his arm. It was a brief contact, stopped almost as soon as it was made, and for a moment the two men's eyes met in a deadlock. Then Kreiger smiled. "You're a real hardass, aren't you?"

Dave said nothing.

"I'll tell you what, detective. I'm taking you with me to meet the woman, but for one reason only. You've seen her; I haven't. She's probably seen you, and might trust you. No black and whites, we're not drawing any attention to ourselves. And we do this my way."

Dave said, "We're wasting time." He moved through the door.

Cathy replaced the receiver and leaned her forehead against the cool plastic casing of the telephone, weak with relief. The worst was over. Help was on its way. They were coming for her and she would be safe.

The telephone booth was an old fashioned one, with a light that came on when the doors were closed. As she lifted her head and drew a shaky breath she saw that the blood splatters on her arms were clearly visible in the light. She began to scrub at them with the hem of her nightshirt, and suddenly she felt exposed, trapped, a vulnerable target to anyone who happened to pass by. How long would it take the police to get here?

She tried to tell herself the maniac on the road was just that—a lunatic, an aberration, a crazy man who spotted a lone woman on the road and thought he would have some fun. She had outwitted him, and that was that. He wouldn't follow her, he wouldn't try to find her . . .

But she hadn't outwitted him. She had escaped him through luck, pure and simple. She had been too startled to brake, too scared to think, and too stupid to know that trying to go around him at full speed was suicidal. The Honda had been narrow enough to squeeze by, and the shoulder had been wider than he expected. He must have been as surprised as she was when she got away. Could she expect to be that lucky again?

Uneasily, Cathy looked around the deserted parking lot. What if he was angry enough to try to follow her? What if he figured out that she had turned left instead of right, and what if he drove by and saw her, pinned in the spotlight of this telephone booth . . .

Don't get paranoid, Cathy, she told herself. *Things are bad enough without you going off the deep end* . . .

But a picture of Jack's face surfaced. It had that sad, puzzled, and slightly reluctant expression he sometimes got when forced to confront an issue he didn't like, or to take a stand that shouldn't have been right, but was necessary.

They had been discussing gun control, one of

51

those issues that had seemed to justify a passionate stand during their college years but that, as one grew older, often faded into insignificance. Jack had surprised her by saying, with that uncomfortable, wishing-it-weren't-so look on his face, "Sometimes the world isn't a nice place, Cath. Whether we like it or not, I guess we've got to be prepared for the worst."

But her world had always been a nice place. And Cathy had never bought a gun.

She slipped out of the telephone booth and left the door open, extinguishing the light. Nothing moved on the street in front of her, but the parking lot was full of shadows. She was alone, vulnerable, and *sometimes the world is not a nice place, Cath.*

If the man in the gray sedan passed by he would spot her car immediately. And if he got here before the police did . . .

What if she hadn't described her location well enough over the phone? What if the police couldn't find her? What if . . .

No. The police would find her. The woman on the phone had told her to stay put. The police would come with sirens blaring and lights flashing, and then she would be safe. But in the meantime, she couldn't stand here in a dark parking lot, waiting for the worst to happen.

She got quickly into the car and started the engine. Across the street, in the school parking lot, there was a fleet of buses drawn up behind the building. Cathy felt a little foolish as she wedged the Honda between two buses where, even if someone were looking, it would be hard to spot. But then she heard Jack's voice again. *We've got to be prepared for the worst.* She would be prepared. She would take no chances, not with what was at stake, not with Jack needing her, waiting for her . . .

She got out of the car and walked around the side of the building, keeping well within the shadows. From there she could watch for the police, but no one could see her.

She had barely reached the corner of the school building when the sound of an approaching car made her stiffen. Instinctively she crouched down, shielding herself behind a leafy bush as the car rounded the curve and the headlights flashed momentarily toward her.

It wasn't the police. It was a blue sedan, slowing its speed as it approached the supermarket on the left. The car turned abruptly into the parking lot, and just for an instant, profiled by the glow of the overhead street light, Cathy could clearly see two men inside.

"Oh, God," Cathy whispered. She brought a shaking hand to her lips and closed her eyes tightly, hoping that when she opened them the car would be gone, or it would be different and she would find that only her overwrought imagination had made her think she had seen it at all.

She opened her eyes again, and the car was still there, pulling close to the telephone booth and stopping. And there was no mistake. The man on the driver's side was wearing a red fishing hat.

"Shit," Dave said softly. He stopped the car, but kept the engine running. The parking lot was big, and dark and empty. If she had ever been here at all she was gone now. And who knew what was waiting for them in her place.

Kreiger commented, "Looks like the lady can't make up her mind."

Kreiger seemed unsurprised, which irritated Dave. Nothing seemed to ruffle the man, or disturb him in the least.

Dave said, "She told Anne she was being followed. Maybe he caught her."

"Or maybe this is a trap."

Dave had been thinking the same thing since he had pulled into the lot and found it empty. And there was only one way to find out.

His heart was beating hard as he pulled out his weapon and got out of the car. Kreiger pulled a .44 magnum out of his shoulder holster and followed.

They circled the parking lot in silence, tense and expectant, pausing at every doorway and shadow. In the back, Dave covered Kreiger while he checked the dumpster and the loading dock. The muscles at the back of Dave's neck were knotted as they returned to the car. The absence of action loomed over him like a cocked gun.

"Who was following her?" Dave said.

Kreiger was gazing across the street, at the deserted school building. "I don't think Delcastle would send her out on her own. He would have had somebody watch her."

"Then why is she running? If it's one of her own men, why is she so scared?"

"Maybe she's not. Maybe she's been lying to you from the first, trying to draw you out."

"Makes no sense." But Toby was dead. Dave swallowed hard.

"Since when did this game have to make sense?" Kreiger shrugged. "My guess is Delcastle found out she was ready to turn and sent one of his tough boys to bring her in. Maybe that's what Clemmons was trying to warn her about, and why she spooked. Make sense enough for you?"

Dave said, "It's only been ten minutes since she called. She can't have gotten far."

They got into the car.

Cathy watched the two men circle the parking lot, guns drawn, looking for her. They were crouched, their postures alert, and they looked ready to shoot anything that moved. She didn't want to believe what she was seeing, but she had to. Somehow the man in the red hat had found her. And he meant to kill her.

For perhaps three minutes, as she watched, she kept expecting to hear the sound of sirens and see the blue lights of rescue stab through the night. But gradually the truth came to her: the police weren't coming. She had called the police and *these* men had come instead. Somehow her phone call had been diverted, or traced, and the very man she had started out fleeing from had come straight to her . . .

Or maybe they *were* the police. The thought flitted across her mind, and she wanted to hold on to it, to infuse it with some hope. Maybe they were undercover, maybe there were things she didn't understand, maybe if she stood up now and called out to them they would put their guns away and take her to a bright, busy police station where she would be safe and everything would be all right. But maybe they wouldn't. Maybe they would start shooting. Maybe they would come over and *tell* her everything was going to be all right, and then put a bullet in the back of her head and hide her body in the trunk of her car and drive it into a river.

Think, Cathy, Jack would have said. *Don't take foolish chances. Be safe.*

So she crouched there, watching, while the blond-haired man stood across the street and seemed to stare right at her. Her fingers were pressed to her lips and her heartbeat was shaking her whole body. Although she knew they couldn't possibly see her from there, she expected the blond man to start moving toward her at any minute, and she was too frightened to even run away. She wanted to sob out loud with despair and frustration but she dared not make a sound, she tried to not even breathe. Terror burned in her chest and tears clogged up her throat as she huddled there behind the bush, praying they would go away.

She didn't know how this had happened, she didn't know who they were. She didn't want to know, she didn't care. Jack was the mystery buff in the family; he read all the crime novels and watched the cop shows. He would have had a dozen theories about what was going on. Jack could analyze things, reason them out, make sense of the most tangled sequence of events. But Jack wasn't here. And Cathy had to do the best she could.

Even when the two men got in their car and drove away, she did not relax. She did not move. They were looking for her, she knew that. Maybe they would think to check the school, maybe they wouldn't. But if she moved, they would surely find her.

She made herself wait a full ten minutes, until she was sure they wouldn't return, then she got in her car. She did not give in to tears, or to the nausea that was threatening to choke her, or to another attack of convulsive trembling. She simply put the car in gear, and drove away.

Chapter Five

After fifteen minutes Dave knew they weren't going to find her. Perhaps he had known before they even started to search; anyone who had eluded police twice was not likely to be found on a cold trail with a ten minute head start. What puzzled him — and perhaps it was the only question he hoped to answer with the search — was *why*. Why call for help and then run before it got there? She said someone was after her. Had he found her? If he hadn't, why hadn't she called again? If he had . . . if he had, it was a pretty sure bet they would never know what happened to her, assuming Kreiger was right about the kind of people she was involved with.

Dave hoped she hadn't been caught, because he needed to know what happened to her. He needed to know a lot of things, and only she could give him the answers. If the need had not been so fierce, so desperate, he would have given up the chase five minutes after leaving the shopping center parking lot.

Kreiger murmured, "Either the lady has picked up some professional tricks, or she's got some professional help. We're not going to find her."

Dave said, "Looks that way." But he would rather deal with a professional than a scared amateur any day. Amateurs were unpredictable, irrational, and more times than not motivated by things a lawman couldn't understand. It was hard to think like an amateur, and being able to think like the enemy was sometimes the only advantage the good guys had. This woman was beginning to look very much like an amateur, and that disturbed him.

Dave pulled into the overgrown drive of Two Mile Church, a gabled wooden structure that fifty years ago had been the subject of more paintings and photographs than Carmel and Big Sur put together. But weather and neglect had taken their toll, and except for the occasional teenage couple looking for romance, and the patrol cars that used it as a turnaround point, no one ever came there anymore.

Dave made the horseshoe turn and put the car in neutral, facing the road. "This is the end of my leash," he said. "Windsor County will pick it up from here. We've got a strict policy about crossing county lines without authorization." And he looked at Kreiger, knowing what the answer would be before he spoke. "Are you authorizing?"

Kreiger said, "Let's go back to the station. I'll take it alone from here."

Dave kept his voice neutral. "That's a lot of lost time."

"And you're wasting more of it."

"All right, Kreiger," Dave said quietly. "Why don't you just stop wasting everybody's time and tell me what's going on here? Because you sure as hell —"

Dave heard his own call letters in the murmur of background static from his radio, and he knew it could only be one thing. He snatched up the microphone.

"Yeah, Dispatch, what've you got?"

"Word from DMV," Anne's voice returned. "The car is registered to Cathy Hamilton, Lynn Haven, California. No warrants, no arrests, no violations. Occupation . . ." Now Anne's voice took on a puzzled tone, "school teacher."

A cold, sinking feeling formed in the pit of Dave's stomach. "Stolen?"

"No report. And we called up the description from Cathy Hamilton's driver's license. It matches the woman at the shooting."

Dave stared at Kreiger. "Shit," he said.

Kreiger's face remained absolutely expressionless — unsurprised, unconcerned, unreactive. It could have been carved from wax.

Dave said softly, measuring each word as it was spoken, "We've got the wrong woman. It's not Laura at all. *We've got the wrong woman.*"

Kreiger said nothing.

"Dave, do you copy? Do you have anything?"

Dave pushed the button on the microphone.

"Copy, Dispatch. We're coming in."

He shoved the car into gear and left a spray of dust behind as he pulled onto the road.

Cathy was lost. With a peculiar apathy that had to be the beginning of deep shock, she registered the fact and didn't care. The winding country road she followed was dark and empty, and looked as though it could go on forever without once intersecting with civilization. She wasn't sure whether she was going north or south, toward the freeway or away from it. Once, another car had appeared on the road, and she had taken a reckless left turn to avoid it — then because she was afraid the driver might have seen the maneuver and followed, she'd turned right at the first chance. Even if she had known where she wanted to be, she couldn't have retraced her steps to get there.

She glanced at the gas gauge. Still a quarter of a tank. Her throat was dry. This far out in the country there were no guarantees about all-night service stations. There were no guarantees about service stations at all. What if . . .

But she didn't let her mind finish that question. There was a far more urgent question, and it had been rising up on the edge of hysteria, like waves of swelling and receding bile, periodically since she had climbed back into the car and started the engine. *Why? Dear God, why is this happening to me?*

What had she done, what did those people want

with her, who were they, how had they found her? What had she done to deserve any of this?

Fortunately, Jack used to say with a twinkle in his eyes, *we hardly ever get what we deserve.* Cathy felt a sudden hysterical urge to laugh, and suppressed it violently. No hysteria, no tears. She had to concentrate, to think. Jack was depending on her now. The children . . .

But no. She couldn't think about the children now. She couldn't think about any of that. She had to *concentrate.*

She glanced again at the gas gauge, and then at the speedometer. Twenty-five miles per hour. Her foot was barely on the gas pedal and she hadn't the energy to press harder. Her control over the car was a fragile thing as it was, just as fragile as her control over her senses. She dared not push any harder.

The landscape on either side of her was tangled and dark, narrow embankments crowded with undergrowth and scrub trees. If there were houses back there she would not be able to see them from here. She needed help. She needed directions. She needed to stop and gather her thoughts and *think* what to do.

Up ahead she saw the profile of a building, tall and weatherbeaten, its wooden steeple leaning drunkenly, sickeningly familiar. She had been this way before. She was going around in circles.

Stop it. Get hold of yourself. You can't just keep driving around using up gas, not even knowing where you are or where you're going. You've got to get out of here, away from this town, away from this county, away from whoever is chasing you. Find the interstate, get away from here, then call the state police or . . . no, just keep going. Find Jack.

Cathy pulled into the cleared-out spot that served as a drive in front of the church, and put the car in park. Around her the churchyard was a study in shadows and darkness, one blending into the other to form blacker shades of gray. Anything could be hiding in those shadows. The windows of the church were black slashes in a scarred gray facade, gaping like open mouths. Anyone could be inside, watching her. Scrub pine and tangled vines formed a living barrier on three sides. The night was deathly still; there was no sound above the car engine, but she strained to hear what wasn't there, to see what wasn't visible.

She tried to take a deep breath, but it caught in her throat. Every nerve in her body felt like a live wire, acting and reacting to stimuli that weren't even there. Her heart was beating too fast, and the nausea of residual terror was thick in her stomach. A thousand eyes were watching her from the darkness, she could feel them. A thousand sounds, muffled by the hum of the engine and the roar of her heartbeat, conspired in the darkness as danger moved closer with every breath. She couldn't stay here. *She couldn't.*

Don't panic. Jack's voice again. *Panic is your worst enemy. Calm down. Think.*

This time, when she tried to take a breath she

almost completed it. Her hands were cold and damp, but they weren't shaking quite as much as they had been a moment ago. She unlatched the map compartment and drew out a map of the Pacific Northwest. It was left over from the drive down from Seattle, three years ago, when she had first come to live with Jack after Lydia deserted her family, leaving Jack with a broken heart and young twins to raise alone. Three years? It was a lifetime ago — a lifetime Cathy didn't even remember, because nothing existed before the telephone call in the middle of the night that had sent her on this journey into hell . . .

She spread the map over the passenger seat, but she couldn't see in the dark, and she dared not turn on the interior light. She fumbled around in her purse until she found a pen light, useful for reading theater programs in the dark. She could not remember the last time she had been to a theater. She pushed the button without much hope, and was rewarded with a faint beam of light. Holding her breath, she focused the light on the map.

She tried to remember the last road sign she had seen, a road number or street name, the last town she had passed through . . . Portersville. Wasn't that the name of the elementary school where she had hidden? She couldn't remember another town name. She tried to trace her route from Lynn Haven, but it was hopeless to try to figure out where she was now. What she needed to do was find the most direct route to the interstate and memorize it. She had to focus, concentrate. Jack was depending on her. She could do this.

She took another breath and brought the wavering light up to the index portion of the map. If she could only find Portersville . . .

Suddenly there was a sharp crack against her window, and a blinding light stabbed her eyes.

Hayforth said thoughtfully, "Well, that explains a few things anyway. Like why she ran."

"Yeah, I'd say so." Dave sat at his desk, absently watching the dots made by his ballpoint pen on the blotter as it slid through his fingers slowly, rhythmically, time after time. "And like the fact that this whole operation's been one screw up after another from the word go. An innocent citizen stops to make a telephone call and two people are dead." The tip of the pen bounced off the blotter once, twice. "Great public servants, huh?"

He tried not to play the what-if game; that kind of mental self-torture was for the rookies. But tonight it kept sneaking up on him. What if she had picked another phone booth? Would the real Laura have eventually shown up? Would everything have been played out exactly the same, or would Toby still be alive? And what if they had had a better description of Laura? What if they—hell, what if *he*—hadn't been so quick to assume? A simple operation, a thousand variables.

All she wanted to do was make a phone call. How could something so easy go so very wrong?

65

Kreiger said, "Not so innocent."

Dave looked up at him, slowly. The pen struck the blotter again. And again. Kreiger was standing at the next desk, bent over a fold-out map of the county that was spread over the top of the desk. Those were the first words he had spoken, except on the phone, since they'd returned to the station.

Hayforth looked reluctant as he agreed, "He's right, Dave. We don't know for sure that she wasn't a plant. That she didn't take Laura's place, or that she *isn't* Laura and the whole thing is some kind of setup."

But he knew it wasn't, just as Dave knew it, deep in his gut where a man was never wrong. Cathy Hamilton was a twenty-nine year-old school teacher from a little town down the coast that nobody had ever heard of, whose only crime had been to stop in Portersville at one-thirty in the morning to use the phone.

Kreiger said. "Whether she is or not, it doesn't matter now."

The pen hesitated above the blotter, but Kreiger's attention had returned to the map. "She picked up that phone," he said, without glancing at them. "We've got to assume she's walking around right now with a head full of information that she doesn't need—and we do."

It was information, Dave acknowledged to himself, that could get her killed.

He demanded quietly, "Who's after her, Kreiger?"

Kreiger met his eyes then, coolly. All pretenses

were dropped between them; he recognized the challenge and met it. "I don't know. You want a guess, it's one of Delcastle's men."

"If anybody knows she's not Laura, it would be Delcastle's own man. Why would he want to kill a stranger?"

He turned back to the map. "Who said anything about killing her? He may just want what we want — information."

"She said he was trying to kill her. On the phone."

Kreiger shrugged. "She's scared. What does she know?"

The tip of the pen struck the blotter, hard.

Hayforth looked at Dave. The two men had worked together for ten years; it wasn't hard for them to guess each other's thoughts.

Hayforth said, before Dave could cut him off, "Your report can wait until morning. Go home, get some rest. It's out of our hands now."

Dave didn't lift his eyes from the pattern of dots on the blotter. The chief was right. It was out of his hands; nothing he could do. The answers he needed, if they came at all, wouldn't be coming from Cathy Hamilton, and they wouldn't be coming tonight.

He said, "Toby's folks. Are they flying in?"

The chief nodded. "It'll be some time in the morning." He hesitated. "They want to take the body with them, back home."

Dave said nothing. He wondered, not for the first time in his life, who would be making those arrangements when his own time came. The force was his only family, and that seemed a sad state of affairs. He had never intended to end up like that, but somehow over the years things had just gotten away from him. His father he had never known, his mother was dead twenty years now, and Alice . . . that was where it had all begun to fade, he supposed. With Alice, who first taught him that life wasn't always fair.

"Chief."

Mathison, the duty officer, was beckoning him across the room, and Hayforth went to him.

Dave slid open the desk drawer to replace the pen, and his eyes fell on a nearly flattened pack of Camels. He had stopped smoking a year ago, after two years of Toby's constant nagging, but he had kept one cigarette—"for an emergency," he'd told Toby. He picked the package up, creasing it between his fingers until the outline of the single cigarette was clearly visible.

Toby, waving away a fog of smoke in the car. "So you want to kill yourself, fine. But don't my lungs get a vote?"

Dave, chuckling as he lit another. "In your line of work, you expect to live forever?"

He held the package a moment longer, then carefully replaced it and slid the drawer shut.

Hayforth was right, there was nothing more he could do tonight. He'd had one chance with Cathy Hamilton, and it was gone. Either they'd pick her up on the APB or they wouldn't, and either way it didn't matter to Dave. She didn't have the answers he needed, she was no longer his concern.

He glanced across at Kreiger, then picked up the phone and dialed the number for long distance information.

"Yeah," he said quietly, "Lynn Haven, California."

A pause, and another voice.

"Cathy Hamilton," he said, "1214 Jordan Street."

He could feel Kreiger's eyes on him as he copied down the telephone number.

Cathy cried out; she couldn't help it. At first she couldn't see anything for the blinding glare in her eyes, but she could hear a man's voice, muffled by the closed window and the sound of the engine. "Open the door! Keep your hands where I can see them and get out quietly, and there won't be any trouble."

After that it all happened very quickly, almost simultaneously: a series of impressions, connections, actions, and reactions that tumbled together so rapidly they almost seemed to be happening outside of her awareness . . . and yet at the same time it was all too slow, too painful, terrifyingly clear. She pushed back in her seat, shading her eyes from the glare, and she caught a glimpse of the man's shadowed form. She heard the click of the door handle and frantically looked at the door lock. It was unlocked. She scrambled for the automatic door lock, but too late, and the door began to swing open. Frantically she tugged at the seat-belt release, twisting around, looking for escape. And that was when she saw the car that had pulled up silently behind her, its presence masked by the sound of her own engine noise. A light green sedan. *The* light green sedan.

She thought, *I can't do this. Jack, don't make me do this . . .*

You have to . . .

This couldn't be happening again. How could it be happening again?

The door was open now, and the flashlight beam swung away as he lunged toward her. That was when she saw in his hand the cool steel of a gun, short and snub nosed, pointed at her.

And that was when the cold, paralyzing horror of disbelief evaporated into fury, whitehot and sharp edged. It wasn't fair. She had done nothing. Her brother was dying—didn't they know that?—his children needed her, she had to get to them because she was all they had and it wasn't *fair*.

She screamed, "I didn't *do* anything!" Her hand, almost of its own volition, grabbed the gear shift lever and slammed it into drive, and her foot stabbed the accelerator. Tires spun, flinging dirt and gravel, and there was a high, thin screaming sound that might have been mechanical, or might have come from her own throat. The car lurched forward and she heard the man's shout—shocked, defiant—and the thump of the car as it struck his body, struck it and made the car swerve with the impact. And then Cathy did scream, because she saw the man's body fly like a broken doll past her eyes and land in the weeds at the side of the drive. She thought, *He's dead, I've killed him, I've killed a man* . . . but she couldn't stop for that now. Some day she would stop and she'd think about it and she'd hear that sound, that dull, bone-cracking *thump* the car made when it hit him. She'd hear it over and over again until she went mad from hearing it . . . but not now. Now she couldn't think about it and now she wasn't sorry.

It was him or you, Cath. You had to.

She swung right out of the drive and onto the road, and as she did the door slammed shut. That sound. She gripped the wheel, dragged in one sobbing breath of air, and pushed down harder on the accelerator.

That sound.

Hayforth said, "The dumpster behind the minimart. They found a woman's body, her throat cut."

Kreiger looked up at him slowly.

Dave said, "Laura?"

Hayforth was looking at Kreiger. "Seems like a bit of a coincidence, doesn't it?"

"It's Delcastle's style," agreed Kreiger. "He found out she was going to turn and he wanted to send you boys a little warning."

"So that's it, then," Hayforth said. His voice was heavy, tired. "We've been chasing the wrong woman." And then his voice sharpened, as though

71

he were focusing his attention, and he looked at Kreiger again. "We're going to need a positive ID. Can you send somebody out to do that?"

Kreiger scowled and made a sharp dismissing gesture with his hand. "No time for that. We've got to bring in the Hamilton woman."

"We've got every patrol car in the state looking for her. If she's out there—"

"That's not good enough! We need choppers, more manpower—"

"If I had it, don't you think I'd use it? Goddamnit, I've got three murders here, and that's about three times as many as I get in a year! *That's* my first priority right now, do you understand that?"

Dave said quietly, "Where was she going?"

Both men looked at him.

"A schoolteacher from Lynn Haven, California . . . What was she doing up here at one-thirty in the morning?"

He looked at the numbers he'd jotted down on the pad, then he picked up the phone and began to dial.

The phone was answered in the middle of the second ring.

"Cathy?" The woman's voice was breathless, anxious.

Kreiger picked up an extension.

Dave said, "This is Detective Dave Jenks, with the Portersville Police Department. Is this the residence of Ms. Catherine Hamilton?"

A sharp indrawn breath, the pain of which

pricked at Dave even across the miles of phone wire. "Oh, no. Please . . . oh, God, what's happened? Is she okay? I knew I shouldn't have let her go alone, she shouldn't have been driving, the state she was in . . . was it an accident? Is she — "

Dave said, "She's all right, ma'am, as far as I know. But she might be in trouble, and I need to ask you some questions. Who am I talking to, please?"

After a moment's hesitation, the voice that came back was tinged with caution, which gradually grew into suspicion and indignation. "This is Ellen Brian, Cathy's friend. . . . Listen, where did you say you were from? Because with what's happened, if you're not calling about Jack you've got a hell of a nerve . . ."

"Who is Jack?"

"Who *are* you?"

"Detective Jenks, Portersville police," Dave repeated patiently. "Miss Brian, your friend drives a red Honda, doesn't she? And she was on her way north?"

The caution was heavy, but the outrage had lessened. "That's right."

"Portersville is about eighty miles north of you. Miss Hamilton stopped here about an hour ago, and there was an incident . . ."

"Oh, for Christ's sake! If you're talking about a traffic ticket or a fender bender — the woman gets a phone call in the middle of the night saying that her brother, her whole family, has been in an accident and they're in a hospital three hundred miles

73

away, so I think you could allow a little—"

"Where?" Dave demanded. "Where are they?"

More alarm than caution now. "Albany. Oregon."

"And that's where she's headed?"

"That's right, but—"

"You said her brother's name was Jack? Jack Hamilton?"

"Yes." The woman's voice was unsteady. "He's in Mercy Hospital in Albany, Oregon, and that's where Cathy was going. . . . Detective, it wasn't just a traffic ticket was it? It was something bad. Is Cathy all right?"

Dave said, "Don't worry, Miss Brian. We're going to do our best to see she gets to Albany safely. Thank you for your help."

Dave returned the phone to its cradle and leaned back in his chair. *Jesus,* he thought. Could it get any worse?

Kreiger ripped the sheet off the notepad where he had jotted down the information Ellen Brian had given them. "All right," he said, his voice taut with satisfaction. "Now at least we know her route. If we don't get her on the road, we have her when she arrives. But this narrows it down to a field we can play in."

Dave looked at him steadily. "Who's after her, Kreiger?"

Kreiger strode toward the door.

Dave called after him, "Do you still want the state patrol to bring her in if they find her first?"

That stopped Kreiger, and he turned, meeting

Dave's eyes for a long moment. Then he said mildly, "Of course."

Dave watched him until he had pushed through the door and disappeared, and still he watched the place he had been, frowning and uneasy.

He couldn't shake the feeling that Cathy Hamilton had been a lot safer when Kreiger was still inside the building.

And who was following her?

Chapter Six

Cathy's parents had died when she and Jack were no older than Jack's twins were now. Cathy had other memories of that age, but the death of her parents was cloudy, indistinct, almost unimportant, as though it were something that had been told to her rather than something she'd experienced. Jack remembered it much better than she did, and he had understood long before Cathy did what "not coming back" meant. For Cathy, it was going to stay at Grandma Floyd's house, with the big oak tree in the yard and the flowered curtains at the windows. She had always loved Grandma Floyd's house. It was like being on holiday all the time, and by the time that holiday feeling faded into what the rest of her life was going to be like, Cathy barely noticed, and never questioned.

Her parents had died in an airplane crash that had taken twelve other lives. Sometimes now, when she heard about a plane crash with loss of life, she would stop and think, *Someone is going to miss them. Someone's life is going to be changed forever.*

Someone isn't coming home, ever again. It was the only way she knew of paying tribute to her parents, because she didn't remember losing them. Their deaths had never touched her.

Growing up had been fairy-tale perfect. Their father had been a real estate developer and he had left his children well provided for; they lacked for nothing. Their maternal grandparents were strong, healthy, and bursting with pride and love. And if ever they felt lonely, out of place . . . they had each other. They had their secret twin signs, they finished each other's sentences, they shared each other's thoughts, for a while they even had their secret twin language, until they realized it was upsetting their grandparents and stopped. They were both bright, outgoing, high achievers, though it was generally acknowledged that Jack was the brightest, the most charming, and would therefore go the farthest. When Cathy looked back on her childhood she couldn't remember anything bad happening to her. Ever.

For her tenth birthday Cathy had received a Persian kitten that she loved beyond all reason. When the cat was a little over a year old it disappeared, and Cathy cried as though her heart would break. But even that story had a happy ending: the next day the cat returned, a little more aloof, a little less eager to purr and cuddle, and those were characteristics it never regained. Otherwise it was none the worse for wear. Not until she was an adult did Cathy learn that the cat had wandered out of the house and been hit by a car; her grandmother, unable to bear Cathy's heartbreak, had substituted another cat of the right

77

appearance and temperament, and the child had never known. Once again, death had brushed close but had not touched her.

And perhaps that was why, even now in the dark, fetid shadow of death's dusty wings, she could not accept the possibility. Jack was not going to die. She was not going to die. The man back in the church-yard was not dead.

He might not be dead. She had gone perhaps three miles when the realization rose up, cold and clear. *How could he be dead?* She had never committed an act of violence against another human being before; she had assumed in her panic and horror that any force would be deadly, but it wasn't. She had struck him with the car going less than ten miles an hour. The sight of that body flying limply past her was imprinted on her brain forever, but if she had looked back would she have seen him struggling to his feet? If she had stopped to check, would she have found him battered and broken, hanging onto life by a thread . . . but still alive?

She couldn't have killed him. It was physically impossible for her to have done so. But she had left him for dead. He might be dead now, or soon . . .

But he had tried to kill her. It had been him or her.

Are you just going to leave him there?

"What am I supposed to do?" Her voice, so ragged and taut with terror it should have been a scream, was little more than a broken whisper. But it was a whisper that filled the interior of the car, echoing around and around and redoubling on itself.

She would be crazy to go back now. Even if she

could find the place again, the man had tried to *kill* her. Hadn't he? The green sedan . . . it *was* the same one. The gun . . . she *had* seen it. And did it matter? Whatever his intentions had been toward her, she was the one who had committed the violence, and if she left him, if he died . . .

Her hands tightened on the steering wheel, bone white. The dryness in her throat went all the way down to her stomach, and it was hard to breathe. *Just let me get out of here. God, please, let this be over . . .*

She tried to think, to concentrate on her driving, on planning a sensible route. The signpost up ahead said Highway 11 and the designation looked familiar; she might have seen it on the map. She took the turn, relaxing just a fraction with the knowledge that now, at least, she knew what highway she was on. She would stop and check the map after a while.

That man . . .

But she wouldn't think about it. Her fingers tightened; she concentrated fiercely.

The quality of the night seemed to change somewhat, fading into a lighter shade of black. It took Cathy a moment to understand what that might indicate. Lights. Civilization. Perhaps even the freeway.

But it was nothing so glamorous. A cluster of roadside shops, all closed now, illuminated by a faded streetlight. A couple of junk shops, a second-hand clothing store. Her headlights flashed off the windows and left them dark again.

A hundred yards ahead was a gas station. It was closed, but there was a phone stand outside.

Her muscles tightened, and she gripped the wheel as though to physically prevent herself from being dragged from the car. She thought, *No. I'm not stopping. I'd be crazy to stop.*

Can you live with yourself if you don't? It seemed like Jack's voice.

No, don't make me do this. Don't . . .

She turned into the parking lot of the service station, close to the phone booth. *Déjà vu.* She put the car in park but left the engine running. Then she sat there, trembling, afraid to move, afraid even to look around at what might be waiting there in the shadows. She couldn't do this. Why did she think she had to do this?

Because, she could almost hear Jack say, *sometimes the line that separates the good guys from the bad guys is the only thing that's clear. Don't blur it now, Cathy.*

She caught her breath and clenched her fists briefly, tightly, digging her nails into her palms to stop the shaking. Then she reached for her purse and tried to find a quarter.

She got out on the passenger side and left the door open, the engine running. The pavement was damp and foggy and her sneakered footsteps echoed when they struck it. Two-and-a-half steps to the telephone. The car door open and welcoming, three feet away. Behind her, the faded clapboard facade of the gas station looked decrepit, abandoned, a sheltering haven for rats or vagabonds or watching eyes. The two pumps were old fashioned, and looked unused. Maybe the place was abandoned. Maybe the phone didn't work. Maybe . . .

She lifted the receiver and heard a dial tone. She dialed 911.

She had no idea what county she was in, what street, what church she had left the victim at. She might have been talking to the same dispatcher she had called before, she didn't know. And she was taking no chances.

When the woman answered, "Emergency," Cathy took a breath and made her voice steady.

"There's an abandoned church with gables and a leaning steeple," she said. "There's been an accident there and a man's hurt. Please hurry."

She replaced the receiver quickly and then brought her fingers to her lips, breathing lightly, shallowly through them while a wave of dizziness passed. Then, before she lost her courage, she lifted the receiver again and dialed another series of numbers.

An eternity passed. The engine hummed beside her, using up precious gas, filling the air with exhaust fumes. Something crackled in the weeds to her right and startled Cathy so badly that she almost ran for the car. But in the next instant, something with small, luminous eyes darted toward the woods, and then the operator answered.

"Yes," Cathy said quickly, "this is collect from Cathy." Her eyes scanned the darkness and she didn't add, *please hurry* though she wanted to. Her skin was tight, prickled with anxiety.

One ring. Two.

"Ellen," she murmured, pressing the phone tighter against her cheek as though to communicate the urgency through it. "Please . . ."

Ellen's voice. "Hello?"

"Ellen, thank God—"

The operator: "This is a collect call from Cathy. Will you—"

Ellen cried, "Yes! I'll accept! Cathy, where are you?"

And for a moment the relief was so acute—the sound of a familiar voice, of normalcy, of a world that hadn't gone completely mad—that Cathy's throat flooded and her knees went weak and she couldn't say anything else.

"Cathy! Is that you?"

Cathy nodded mutely, trying not to sob.

"Cathy, thank God! Are you all right? Where are you?"

"Oh, Ellen, it's been so awful, and I'm so scared . . ." Cathy's voice was thick and she drew a hand over her wet face. "I can't—I don't know where I am, and I'm almost out of gas, and Jack . . ."

"Cathy." Ellen's voice was sharp with anxiety. "Cathy, this policeman called here looking for you, a detective. He said you were in some kind of trouble. Cathy, what's wrong?"

Abruptly, Cathy's tears dried, as though they were sucked into the cold cavity that had suddenly opened up in her chest. "Somebody called—looking for me? Called my home?"

"A detective, he said. I wrote his name down somewhere. Wait a minute . . ."

"What did you tell him?"

"Why . . . the truth. That you drove a red car and you were on your way to see Jack, and about the accident, and . . . I did the right thing, didn't I? You'd want me to do that, wouldn't you?"

Cathy stared into the darkness, trying to think, trying to make sense of it, trying to plan. "Yes. Yes, of course you did, Ellen . . ."

"Cathy, you're scaring me. Tell me what's happened. Do you need me to come get you? Where are you?"

Yes! she wanted to cry. *Come get me, take me away from here, do something, help me* . . . But twice, not counting the time at the mini-mart, someone had tried to kill her. How could she put Ellen in the same danger? Besides, by the time she got here it might be too late.

She said, "No. I can't—" She pushed her hair back from her forehead, drawing a breath, trying to think. "I can't tell you about it now. I have to—let me find a better place, and call you back." The police, she thought. Ellen could call the police . . . But when Cathy had called the police the enemy had shown up. Now the police were calling Ellen, and Cathy had done nothing. *Nothing.* Where was the line now between the good guys and the bad guys?

She said, "The hospital. Jack. Have you heard anything?"

"No. I'm going to call them now. Cathy, why don't you stop someplace for the night? Let me meet you there, and we'll drive the rest of the way together in the morning. You don't sound good at all, and I'm worried . . ."

Cathy heard the distant sound of tires on the road, and every muscle in her body tightened with adrenaline. "No. I can't stop, I can't talk now. Lis-

ten Ellen, I—call the hospital, I'll call you back . . .
I have to go."

She hung up the phone without saying goodbye.
The sound of tires was closer, now she could hear
engine noise. Her heart pounding, she scrambled inside the car and slammed the door shut. She pressed
herself flat across the front seat just as the interior
was illuminated by the flash of headlights . . . that
was gone in an instant as the automobile sped by.

And still Cathy stayed there, her heartbeat shaking her entire body, while she imagined the car stopping, backing up, coming back to her . . .

It didn't. And at last Cathy pushed herself into a
sitting position, slid across the seat, and took the
wheel again.

In 1987, after a heavy rain that followed a long
drought, the earthen dam north of town had broken, plunging streets and highways six feet under
water in a matter of minutes, leaving hundreds
homeless and injuring dozens. Since that time,
Dave could not remember the station being as fran-
tic as it was now.

Except on weekends and holidays, Portersville all
but closed down after dark. The chief kept on a skel-
eton crew from midnight to six A.M.—two patrol
cars and the watch commander. Tonight, because it
was routine to have backup standing by on a raid or
a bust, the complement was somewhat heavier. But
after the shooting, it looked as though every officer
in Portersville had come in, some in uniform and
some in civvies, all of them ready to do what had to

be done. One of their own was dead. They couldn't stay at home and pretend this was an ordinary night.

And neither could Dave.

He wanted to. He wanted to go home and sit blank-eyed with an open bottle of Jack Daniels and think nothing at all for the rest of the night, well into the morning, and most of the next day. Then, when he was as drunk as he could possibly get and still stay conscious, he would think about it.

That was what he wanted to do. And because he wanted it so badly, he stayed right where he was. He didn't try to take over the case, he didn't demand an assignment or insist on a chance to avenge his partner, as another man might have done. He sat at his desk and stayed quiet, pretending to work on his report, listening, evaluating, and thinking. What he thought about, mostly, was Cathy Hamilton.

It was easy to lose yourself in the routine of a place like Portersville, which was why Dave liked it so much. Teenage shoplifting, the occasional burglary, the odd obscenity or pandering violation . . . nothing he couldn't leave behind at the end of the shift, nothing to worry a man over dinner or keep him up after the "Tonight" show. Portersville was not so small that he knew every citizen personally, and not so large that it attracted the big-time nature of gruesome crimes, and Dave liked it like that. There was nothing to tempt a man to get emotionally involved in his work. It had been eight years since Dave had been emotionally involved with anything, and that was another thing he had liked about his life. Until now.

He knew about the phone call in the night. If it

hadn't been for that part of the story he probably could have wiped Cathy Hamilton out of his mind as just another victim. She wasn't part of his case, even if there had been a case. She wasn't going to lead him to the reason his partner had died, she wasn't going to put any bad guys behind bars; she had troubles of her own, and so did Dave. She was just another innocent bystander caught up in the system, and he could have forgotten her—he had trained himself to forget—if it hadn't been for that phone call. The one that drew a line down the center of your life and changed what you were, deep inside, where it counted, forever.

He glanced down at the legal pad where he had absentmindedly drawn a series of squares around the words "Mercy Hospital," so that now the name was surrounded by a bold black frame. From the frame an arrow pointed to the words "Jack Hamilton." Her brother.

Midnight, one o'clock in the morning, stumbling out of bed with your heart pounding, stunned, sick . . . *She's asking for you. Hurry* . . . Plunging out into the night, shaking hands turning the key in the ignition, driving without looking at the road or even recognizing it, just hoping the car would get you there before it was too late. The phone call. He knew it.

"I thought I told you to go home."

Dave grunted acknowledgment without glancing up. It was the chief. He dropped his eyes back to the legal pad, where he was beginning to draw the same geometric frame around Jack Hamilton's name. He said thoughtfully, "He wasn't surprised we had the wrong woman."

Hayforth frowned. "What?"

"Kreiger. He wasn't surprised when the DMV report came in. And he didn't seem too interested in that woman in the dumpster, did he? If this was your case, and your key witness showed up in a dumpster with her throat cut, don't you think you'd at least be interested?"

"Laura wasn't his witness, she was ours. He was sent to set up the bust, and to do that he's got to know when and where. The only one who can tell him that is the Hamilton woman. SOP. What are you driving at?"

Dave still didn't look up. *"He* could have ordered choppers, roadblocks. The federal budget hasn't been cut that short."

This time there was a silence before Hayforth answered, and when Dave glanced up it was to see he wasn't the only one who had had that thought. "I've got a call in to Washington," he said. "It might be morning before we get an answer."

"Meanwhile . . ."

"Meanwhile," replied Hayforth firmly, "it's not our case."

Dave dropped his eyes back to the pad. He added another square to the frame around Jack's name. Her whole family, Ellen Brian had said. Did they live in Oregon, or were they just traveling through? Her brother and her parents, her brother and his wife and children . . . ?

None of your business. Not your case.

He said, "All right, our case. Who killed Laura? If it was Laura. Have we ID'd her yet?"

"Working on it."

"And Clemmons. Who was he, what was he do-ing there, why did he open fire? Do you buy Kreiger's story?"

Hayforth looked wary. "You've got a reason not to?"

"Just one. If he worked for Delcastle, if he was sent to warn Laura off, it stands to reason he would've known what she looked like. Don't you think?"

Hayforth said quietly, "Yeah, I think. But it wouldn't be the first time I've been wrong, or you either, so that doesn't make a working theory. You know the policy here, Dave, or maybe you don't, be-cause it's been a long time since we had to enforce it. As soon as you turn in your report you've got a week's compassionate leave coming, then two weeks' desk duty. There's nothing more for you to do here." His voice gentled as he touched Dave's shoulder awkwardly. "Finish up in the morning."

And suddenly Dave understood. Hayforth was remembering what had happened after Alice died. He was waiting—everyone was waiting—for him to fall apart.

All Dave could do was look his boss in the eye and say, "I'm okay, Chief." Even though it was a lie and they both knew it, Dave thought Hayforth wanted to believe it almost as much as he did.

Hayforth started to turn away, but was stopped by Thompson, an off-duty uniform who had come in without being asked. He said, "Kelsey and Jordan responded to an anonymous tip about an accident at Two Mile Church. They just called in. The victim

88

identified himself as an FBI agent assigned to the Kreiger case. I think you'd better get out there, sir.

"Jesus Christ," said Hayforth, but he was already moving toward the door.

Dave was right behind him, and Hayforth didn't try to stop him.

They arrived approximately three minutes after the ambulance. Dave noticed the stunned, taut look on the faces of the EMTs and he knew what they were feeling. Chokings, drownings, traffic accidents—they saw their share of action. But in the past hour or so they had been called to two murders and now a hit and run. That wasn't in the manual, not for a place like Portersville.

Sorry about that, boys, Dave thought as he followed Hayforth quickly across the rutted drive. *That's what happens when you don't keep your eye on the ball.*

Dave noticed the green sedan in passing. It was parked in the shadows and didn't look damaged. The victim was sitting up in the back of the ambulance, so apparently he wasn't too badly damaged either. Hayforth edged his way around the technicians and identified himself.

"Special Agent Joe Frazier." The words were uttered tightly through teeth set in pain. He passed Hayforth his badge. "I need to call my superior."

Dave glanced at the badge over Hayforth's shoulder. "You working alone?"

Frazier sucked in his breath as one of the paramedics wrapped an inflatable splint around his arm.

It was broken, and from his posture Dave guessed a couple of ribs were as well. A scrape on the side of his face was matted with blood and his shirt was torn; Dave's guess was that he was out of commission for the duration of this case, anyway.

He said briefly, "I am now."

Hayforth returned the badge. "Tell me what you know about the shooting."

"I don't think you need to know the details of our operation. If you'll just — "

"*I'*ll tell you what I need to know!" Hayforth took a swift, furious step toward Frazier. "It's three o'clock in the morning and I'm up to my knees in ~~fucking~~ dead bodies, and what I need to know is what the ~~fuck~~ *you're* doing in my town ~~fucking~~ up my night's sleep. Have you got that?"

"Chief," one of the paramedics said tightly as he pressed Frazier back down into his seat, "if you'll just give us a minute."

But Hayforth didn't back down and Frazier locked eyes with him, stubborn anger tightening the muscle in his jaw that was already knotted with pain.

Dave said, "Who was your partner?"

Reluctantly, Frazier moved his eyes away from Hayforth and onto Dave. The hatred Dave saw there startled him. Frazier said, "Deke Clemmons. The man you killed."

Jack was a professor of English literature at Carlton, a small private college twelve miles away from Lynn Haven. He had written his thesis on

90

Yeats and had published two papers on Elizabeth Barrett Browning, but when he picked up a book to read it was generally a spy novel or an intricately plotted political thriller, the kind of thing Cathy could never understand but that Jack devoured like cotton candy. He would have liked what was happening now, if it were written into a novel. He would have understood it. If it were a television show he would be pointing at the screen and saying, "See, Cath, what's going to happen now is . . ."

But Cathy's imagination wouldn't supply the next words. She didn't know what was going to happen now. She didn't understand what had happened so far. Who was that man in the green car? How had the police gotten her home phone number? Why had they called Ellen?

God, why hadn't she *asked* Ellen that? Why hadn't she asked what the detective had wanted?

Maybe she should turn herself in. If the police were looking for her, maybe the safest thing she could do would be to just stop and call them, and . . .

But she hadn't *done* anything! The last time she had called the police two men with guns had come, one of whom she had last seen pointing that very gun at her face. Something was wrong here, very wrong, but she couldn't figure it out. Jack would know. But he wasn't here, he was lying in a hospital bed, broken and hurting, waiting for her . . .

"Oh, Jack," she whispered. "I'm trying. I hope I've done the right things, because I'm trying . . ."

And then, like an answer to a prayer or a sign from heaven, her headlights picked up the small blue-and-white sign that announced the upcoming interstate. A wave of gratitude went through her that burned her eyes and weakened her muscles.

"Yes," she whispered, blinking hard to clear her eyes. "Oh, yes."

She put on her signal indicator and made the turn.

Dave said, "Shit." His head swam and he felt sick inside—not only from what Frazier had said, but from what it implied. And for the longest time, all he could do was stare at the other man.

Something in his face must have shamed Frazier, though Dave didn't mean to, nor had he any right to, because Frazier eventually shifted his gaze. He said quietly, "Look, I know you were just doing your job. We had no way of knowing locals were tied up in this. By the time I realized—when you identified yourself—my partner was dead and so was yours. All I could do was try to stop the woman."

"So it was you after Cathy Hamilton." It was all Dave could think of to say.

"Is that her name?"

"She's not involved in this, you know. Just a bystander."

Frazier looked confused. The injection the paramedics had given him was beginning to take effect. "No, I didn't know."

"Jesus Christ." Hayforth half turned from him, as though looking away were the only way he could control his temper, then turned back again. "Seems to me like there's a good bit you didn't know, isn't there, Frazier? Do you think the next time you boys decide to sweep down and shoot up a town you could manage to be a little better informed?"

Dave said, "You said you were assigned to the Kreiger case." His stomach was tight, with premonition or certainty. "Since when does the DEA use the FBI as back up?"

Frazier closed his eyes briefly and passed a hand over his sweaty face.

One of the paramedics looked up at Hayforth. "Chief, we're going to have to transport now. You can finish this at the hospital."

"No." Frazier held up a hand. He looked at Hayforth, then at Dave. He said, "He had you working with him, didn't he? What has he done?"

Hayforth said cautiously, for the truth was beginning to dawn on him too, "So far, not much. We've got an all-points out for the Hamilton woman, and he's on the road, following her route."

Frazier nodded tiredly. "Then you'd better hope the state patrol picks her up before he does." His eyes met Dave's, and Dave heard the words almost before they were spoken. "Kreiger's a rogue. We've been watching him set up this deal for months. Everything was going like clockwork until you boys stepped in." There was no accusation in the words, just a statement of fact. "Now he's got us outsmarted and outnumbered, and the only thing that's standing between him and thirty million dollars is that woman in the red Honda."

Dave said, "Did she do this to you?"

Frazier nodded groggily. "Caught me off guard.

Hell, she didn't look like a bystander . . ."

Dave and Hayforth watched as he was moved into the ambulance, strapped onto a stretcher. Then, thoughtfully, Dave walked back to the car and picked up the radio mike.

"Anne. Did you take that anonymous tip about the Two Mile Church accident?"

"I sure did. It came in at 3:03."

"Was it from a woman?"

"Why, yes. It was."

"Thanks. Out." He replaced the mike and straightened up, leaning against the car door, looking out over the highway. The ambulance's taillights flashed in the distance and disappeared over a hill. The road was deserted.

Hayforth said, "I'm going to try to get some more out of him. You want me to drop you back at the station?"

"No. I'll come along for the ride, if you don't mind."

He half-expected Hayforth to refuse. Instead, the other man followed Dave's thoughtful, disturbed gaze down the road. He said, "We can request that the state patrol notify us if they spot her, but for right now, that's about all. Meanwhile . . ."

"Meanwhile," Dave finished quietly, "we hope like hell she stays on the back roads. Because if she makes it to the interstate she's going to be a sitting duck."

He met Hayforth's eyes briefly, then turned and got into the car.

Chapter Seven

The routes that crack cocaine traveled from its point of origin to the streets and byways of middle America were many and varied. It came up the coast from Mexico to distribution points in L.A. or San Francisco, and branched out to Detroit and Chicago. It traveled the Florida highways to Atlanta and on to New York, or filled the holds of private planes that were bound for landing strips in the desert. It was packed into false bottoms of fishing boats or speed boats whose ports of call would eventually touch every city in America.

The systems designed to take the product from its distribution point to the consumer were formulated with the sophistication of Fortune 500 companies: franchises were sold, CEO's assigned, quality control mechanisms in place, security forces trained. The organization assigned to make certain the product did *not* reach the consumer was of necessity at least as sophisticated—state-of-the-art equipment, highly trained technicians, and a vast underground network were only a few of its tools. When the resources of the latter were joined with those of the former, the result was formidable.

That, Joe Frazier explained, was what made Kreiger so dangerous. He was not working alone. He had all the high-tech resources of the United States government behind him, as well as the vast network of one of the most successful businesses in the history of the world. With those factors on his side from the beginning, his chances for success were better than even.

Or they had been, until Cathy Hamilton intercepted that phone call.

"Pull his ticket," Dave insisted when Frazier, still weak from his injuries and groggy with medication, finished his story. "Get him off the goddamn streets. At least cut off his link to the law enforcement network—"

"You know we can't do that," Frazier answered tiredly. "Until he does something outside his duties as a federal agent, we've got suspicions but no case. That's what this whole operation was about: making a case."

"The something he could do," suggested Dave flatly, "is kill Cathy Hamilton."

"He won't kill her. He needs the information she's got too badly."

Dave did not voice the obvious. Cathy Hamilton was expendable. For now she was the bait that would lure the big fish; once Kreiger got the information he needed he may or may not let her live—that was neither the FBI's problem or its responsibility. Two more agents were on their way to Portersville now, but it was unlikely they would arrive before morning. Until then, Cathy Hamilton was the least of their concerns.

As for the Portersville Police Department, they too had bigger problems than Cathy Hamilton. She had never been a part of their case, and now she wasn't even in their jurisdiction. But that wasn't going to make her any less dead when Kreiger got what he wanted from her.

There was no point blaming Frazier, or demanding more information, or pointing out the inequities of the system. Nobody ever said life was fair, and Cathy Hamilton was just one of hundreds — thousands — who fell through the cracks every day.

But before leaving the E.R. cubicle where Frazier was awaiting treatment, Dave turned back. "I'm sorry," he said, "about your partner."

Frazier swallowed hard, and nodded, and averted his eyes. "Hell of a business," he said.

Dave agreed bleakly, "Yeah," and left.

Three-thirty in the morning found him back at his desk, staring at the map on the far wall, wondering where Cathy Hamilton was now. Knowing it was none of his business and not his problem, but wondering.

It's over, Cathy thought. She kept telling herself that, repeating the words in her mind as though by doing so she could make herself believe them. *Over*.

Portersville was thirty-seven miles behind her, but the horror of that place clung to her like a bad odor, rode beside her in the seat, dogged her shadow. The Oregon state line was a hundred miles distant, and maybe when she crossed it this would be over, maybe then she would be safe. If she made it that far.

One thing was certain: she would not make it without a full tank of gas. The needle now hovered just above empty, but the gauge was unreliable below a quarter of a tank. She might have enough gas for fifty miles or five. She couldn't put it off any longer. She had to stop.

The other vehicles on I-5 were few and far between, and Cathy was never sure, when one of them approached her, whether to be grateful or terrified. The big rigs she didn't mind, she even took a kind of comfort in their presence. But since she had gotten on the interstate she had seen five passenger cars, and any one of them could have been following her, plotting to move ahead and cut her off, waiting at the next exit. It wasn't over. It would never be over.

Or so the paranoid part of her mind told her. The other part, struggling to hold onto reason in a world gone mad, assured her that whatever had gone wrong thirty miles down the highway could not follow her here. No one was following her, no one was plotting against her, no one was trying to trap her. But still she let exit after exit go by, gas station after gas station.

I'll stop at the next one, she promised herself,

and her throat went a little dry as she looked down at the gas gauge. *I can make it for one more exit*.

And then she heard the siren behind her, and saw the flash of blue lights.

Since Alice, Dave had not been in a serious relationship. He knew several women and sometimes he dated, but even that was getting to be more trouble than it was worth. Everyone expected too much. Dave expected nothing at all.

His relationships never lasted more than a month or two, not because he planned it that way — or at least he wasn't aware of doing so — but because the women always wanted more. Because they always sensed somehow that secret part of himself he was keeping in reserve. When they started trying to break down that barrier, that was when he had to leave.

The last woman he had left had put it most plainly: "It's not going to bring her back, you know. You can close yourself off and live in the past, but in the end all you're going to be is alone. And what's worse, I don't think she'd want it that way. Do you?"

He knew Alice wouldn't want it that way. Alice was the most passionately committed person he had ever known. She cared about everything, and she cared deeply — about whales, about jazz, about what she was having for dinner, about living. Dave's deliberate lack of the same kind of zeal had been the only thing that ever came between them. He tried to blame it on being a cop. If a man started to care about every hard-luck case that crossed his desk, if he started to get personally involved with every battered wife and abandoned kid and substance abuser he encountered, he wouldn't last long, as either a lawman or a human being. A man had to protect himself.

All right, Alice had insisted, self-protection was allowed. But there had to be some part of him that was free to get involved in something, deeply and passionately, some part of him that could care, without reservation, about someone or something outside himself. So Dave had cared about her, with every ounce of conviction and commitment in his soul, and she had died. It was perhaps the single greatest betrayal in his life.

But he knew she would not approve of the way he had chosen to live his life now. She would not understand how important self-protection had become, how easy it was not to care.

My partner died in my arms tonight, Alice, he thought. *And I killed an innocent man. Now a woman who doesn't understand any of it is out there alone being stalked by an outlaw, and what would you have me do?*

Stupid question. There was nothing he could do. He couldn't be responsible for the whole world, and Cathy Hamilton was out of his hands.

A little after three-thirty he finished his report

and was just getting ready to hand it in when Thompson called to him from across the room. "Hey, Dave, it's the state patrol. They've picked up your girl in Hinesville."

Dave snatched up the receiver. "Yeah, Detective Jenks. Who's this?"

"Lieutenant Forester, CHP. Listen, we've got one Catherine Hamilton in custody. She was stopped on a routine speeding ticket, but we ran it through the computer and this turned up."

Dave offered a silent prayer of relief that something about the system was still working. And then Forester went on. "So what are we holding here? It says something about a shooting, but I need to know what kind of security we're going to need. And what's the involvement with the DEA? We've notified agent Kreiger, but until he gets here—"

Everything within Dave went cold. "What?"

"As per the instructions on the bulletin. What I want to know is—"

"Let her go," Dave said hoarsely. A dozen questions, a hundred demands, were slamming against the top of his head, trying to get out. His hand tightened on the receiver as he struggled for control, for calm. "Don't let him have her."

"What?"

"You heard me." Dave hadn't intended to shout, but his voice was loud enough to make heads turn. "The bulletin was issued from this office and I'm canceling it. You let her go now before that bastard—"

"Hey, wait a minute, detective, I can't do that and you know it. My orders are to release her to Agent Kreiger and no one else. I don't even know why your name was on the bulletin to contact—"

"Because *I* put it there, goddamnit!"

Chief Hayforth was standing by his desk, quietly watching. He didn't have to say anything; Dave knew it all. His fingers tightened on the phone; tightened, and slowly relaxed. The animal, wild and raging, was reluctantly subdued.

"Do me a favor," he said quietly.

The man on the other end sounded disinclined to do anything of the sort. "Yeah? What's that?"

"Let me talk to her. Just bring her up front and put her on the phone for a minute."

There was a hesitance. "That's pretty irregular."

"I know. Just do it. Please."

Another silence, followed by a tone that was more curious than annoyed. "I sure do wish I knew what the hell was going on."

Dave passed a weary hand across his forehead. "No you don't, Lieutenant. No you don't."

No one would tell her, but Cathy thought she understood. She wasn't being held for a minor traffic violation. The trooper who had stopped her said she was speeding, and she probably was, but she knew he had been about to let her go with a warning when the report came through on the computer. He told her there was a warrant out for her arrest. She had protested, she had struggled, she had even—though she hated herself for doing it—cried. She hadn't *done* anything. But someone obviously thought she had. Someone thought she was involved in the shooting back at the minimart.

And she was, she realized slowly. She sat in the holding cell on a cot with one broken leg, with two female companions—a chain-smoker and a sullen DUI—and let the pieces come together. For the first time since the nightmare began she actually had time to be still and think, and it was as though a great smothering fog had suddenly been lifted from her brain. She was guilty. She had fled the scene of a crime. She was a material witness to a murder. Of course the police were looking for her. Of course there was a warrant out for her.

She wrapped her arms around her waist and rocked back and forth, breathing slowly, trying to stop the pounding of her heart. *Jack, I'm sorry* . . .

She tried not to let it overwhelm her. She tried not to think about being alone in a strange town, locked in jail for a crime she wasn't sure she understood; she tried not to think about how much worse it could get; she tried not to think about Jack . . . no, she couldn't think about Jack.

Phone call. They had to allow her a phone call. She'd call Ellen—thank God for Ellen!—who would bring bail money, who would find a lawyer, who would help her get out of here. But what about Jack? It was close to four o'clock in the morning. By the time Ellen got here, by the time

103

she found someone to help her and got Cathy out of jail . . . what about Jack?

What if they wouldn't let her out? Wasn't there some kind of provision about being able to hold a suspect for forty-eight hours before charging him? Hadn't she seen that on television, read about it, hadn't Jack told her? . . . She couldn't stay here forty-eight hours! She felt hysteria rising. What if they tried to take her back to that town Portersville, where it had all started? That's what they would do, of course they would, and they would hold her there as long as the law allowed. But she couldn't go back there. She couldn't stay there, they had to understand. Jack . . .

There were footsteps in the corridor, a gate being unlocked. A uniformed woman came to the cell and turned the key. The blond chain-smoker looked up sharply, but the woman said, "Hamilton. Come with me, please."

Cathy stood on legs that she wasn't entirely sure would support her, and followed the woman out of the cell.

They had reached the front room before Cathy managed to make her voice work. "I need to make a phone call," she said hoarsely.

"You'll get a chance for that. Right now somebody's calling you."

Cathy looked at the woman, startled, but she merely gestured Cathy toward the telephone at an empty desk and stayed very close to her as Cathy moved hesitantly toward it.

She started to pick up the receiver, then hesitated. "Who would be calling me?" she said. "Why would anyone—"

The officer shook her head, but there was the trace of a compassionate smile on her lips. "You've got three minutes," she said.

Cathy picked up the receiver and the officer pushed a button on the phone base. Cathy said hesitantly, "Hello?"

And then she knew, every bone in her body screamed it, something was wrong here. No one should be calling her. No one knew she was here. No one except the man, or men, who were following her. The man who had found out her name and called her house, the man who had drawn his gun in the overgrown parking lot of a deserted church, the men who had responded to her call for help in an unmarked car with guns drawn . . .

A male voice responded, "Cathy Hamilton?"

Cathy, she thought. *He called me Cathy, not Catherine.* That seemed important somehow, but there were other things that were much more important. *They won't believe you. They've come after you with guns twice now, and they won't believe you're innocent if you tell them . . .*

"Yes," she said hoarsely. "Who is this?"

"My name is Dave Jenks. I'm a detective with the Portersville Police Department."

And before she could stop herself she burst out, "I didn't do anything! I swear to you I didn't—"

"We know that, Cathy—"

"Then why are you chasing me? Why am I in jail? Stop lying to me, leave me alone! Why can't you just *leave me alone?*"

It wasn't until she felt the firm grip of the officer's hand on her arm that Cathy realized she was screaming, her breath was harsh and her cheeks were wet with tears. There were three or four other patrolmen in the room, working at their desks, drinking coffee, talking and laughing among themselves. The laughter had stopped and Cathy could feel their eyes on her.

She took a breath, and another. She pressed her lips together and she thought, *I've got to get out of here.*

The voice on the other end of the phone was calm, deliberate. "I know you're scared, Cathy."

"Stop calling me that!" She spat out the words between tightly clenched teeth. She could feel the muscles in her shoulders trembling, she was gripping the telephone so tightly. "You don't know anything about me, you don't know what you've put me through. I haven't done anything, and I *hate* you for what you've put me through!" Then she had to stop and take another breath, because she could feel the edge of control slipping and the officer's hand was very tight on her arm.

His voice didn't change. Calm, measured. In control. "All right. Then listen to me. This is important."

"I have to get out of here," she said, trying, with every fiber of her being, to make her voice as reasonable as his. "You said you know I didn't do anything wrong. You said that. You're going to have to make them let me go. My brother and—

106

and his children are in the hospital, and the babies — I'm their nearest relative. I have to get to them. You've got to help me get out of here."

"We're working on that, but right now you're in the safest place you could possibly be."

She wanted to scream at him, *Working on it? How can you be working on it? I shouldn't be here in the first place and you know that! How can you be working on it?* But she didn't say anything, because she didn't trust herself to release so much as a breath.

"Listen to me, Cathy. Try to understand. You're in a lot of trouble. I'm on your side, but that might not be enough. There's a man on his way to you right now. His name is Scott Kreiger, and he'll probably try to take you into custody. Don't go with him. Don't tell him anything. Do whatever you have to — pretend to be sick, try to escape, make a disturbance — but don't let him take you out of that station house. I'll do what I can from here, but in the meantime stay away from Kreiger. Do you understand?"

Cathy's throat ached with a sudden dryness, and she felt ill. "You're crazy," she said, barely above a whisper. "Don't tell me that. I'm in jail and I've got to get out and — why are you telling me that? How do I know you're not the one who's been trying to kill me? Why should I believe you? Why are you doing this to me?"

For the first time the calm competence in the man's voice wavered, became tinged with an edge of frustration. "I can't make you believe me," he said. "I can't do anything but tell you what I know, and that's what I'm trying to do now." He drew a breath, sharp and long. "All right. Listen. Ask someone for a pencil and a piece of paper. Have you got it?"

Cathy looked around and found a felt-tip pen. The officer tore off a page from a notebook. "Yes."

"Write down my name, and this number." He read off a series of numbers. "Call me if you need help. That's all I can do for you."

"Make them let me go," Cathy pleaded with a sudden burst of desperation, one last time. "You know I'm innocent, tell them to let me go."

For a moment she almost thought she had gotten through to him, that he might be listening to her after all, that she might be saved . . . but all he said was, in a strange, tight tone, "Hold on to that number, Cathy. Use it." And he hung up the phone.

Cathy stood there listening to the dial tone until the officer gently took the felt-tip pen from her hand. Cathy replaced the receiver. *Crazy,* she thought. *This whole thing is crazy* . . . Jack would have enjoyed this: point-counterpoint, warnings from a stranger, danger in the night . . . only Jack would have figured out the plot by now. Jack would know what to do.

She shook herself a little, grasping for the edge of reason. Do? There was only one thing to do. She had to get out of here. She had to call Ellen, she had to get a lawyer. She had to make bail . . .

108

she had to get to Jack. That was all that mattered. She had to get to Jack.

The officer tugged at her arm, her grip more gentle now. "Come on, honey. Back you go."

"But — my phone call — "

"Prisoners don't use the phones up here for their calls. There's a pay phone in back. Come on, now."

"Yes. Okay." With a steadying gulp of breath, Cathy pushed back her hair and let the woman start to lead her away. And then she stopped, and looked back at the desk. After a moment's hesitation, she picked up the paper on which she had scrawled the name and phone number and pushed it into her jeans pocket. Then she nodded to her escort and even tried to smile a little as she was led back toward the cell.

The silence around his desk was thick and heavy, and it was a long time before Dave could make himself break it. "He's going to get her," he said, without looking up. "The son of a bitch is going to get her unless we can get to her before he does."

"Dave, it's not — "

"If you tell me one more time it's not our case . . ." Dave said, very softly.

Hayforth was silent for the time it took to swallow back harsh words. "It's not," he said flatly. "We've got a big enough mess to clean up on our own turf and it's only going to get worse. We don't have the authority to override a federal agent's orders on the Hamilton woman, even if the agent is suspect, and the FBI's not going to thank us for screwing up their case—again. Stay out of it, Dave."

"Screwing up their case," Dave repeated softly. "Yeah, I guess we did that all right. Of course, lucky for them they had an alternate plan. Do you want to know what Plan B is, Chief?" He slid open the desk drawer and took out his gun, checked the clip. "Plan B is to let Kreiger get the information from the girl however he can and keep his rendezvous. The point of the game is to catch him with the goods, and they can't do that if he doesn't know where to go."

Hayforth said quietly, "It's not your business, Dave."

"You got that right." Dave holstered the gun, and his eyes fell on the cigarette pack, flattened up to its single remaining occupant. He picked up the pack and put it in his pocket. If this didn't qualify as an emergency, he supposed nothing ever would.

"That number you gave her—it wasn't your home, it wasn't the station."

"Right."

"Car phone?"

Dave stood up.

Hayforth's next words were studied and deliberate, but Dave read the message in his eyes very clearly. "Don't make me ask for your badge, Dave."

Dave smiled, faintly. "I won't." He picked up

the report on his desk and handed it to the chief. "If anybody asks for me, I'm on compassionate leave. I'm thinking about driving up north, maybe as far as Oregon. Do a little fishing, take in the woods. You probably won't be able to reach me."

Hayforth held his eyes for a long time, then nodded slowly. "I'll tell them. If anybody asks."

Dave lingered a moment longer, but there was nothing left to say. He picked up his windbreaker and pulled it on over the shoulder holster as he moved toward the door.

This one's for you, Alice, he thought, and pushed out into the night.

Chapter Eight

Cathy never got to make her phone call. As they reached the holding area someone called to the woman who was escorting Cathy, the two officers consulted briefly, and before she knew it Cathy was signing a receipt for the return of her purse and its contents.

He did it, she thought dazedly. The man on the phone, the policeman, had come through after all. He had made them let her go. There was a God. Everything was going to be all right.

Then someone said behind her, "Miss Hamilton?"

A tall blond man was approaching. "My name is Scott Kreiger."

He took a folder from his pocket and opened it for her. It contained a badge and a photograph and some kind of official insignia. Cathy stared at it for a long time, her heart pounding.

He said, gesturing, "I wonder if we could step over here where it's quiet and I could ask you a few questions."

Cathy turned back to the man behind the counter. "My car," she managed. Her voice was raspy and thick, as though from overuse.

He passed her a slip of paper. "Just give this to the attendant at the impound yard."

Cathy stared at the paper, trying to make sense of the words printed there. "But—I don't know where this is. How can I get there?"

The phone rang and the man behind the counter reached for it, giving Cathy a disinterested shrug.

Kreiger's voice sounded a little impatient behind her. "Miss Hamilton—"

Cathy's hand clenched on the paper, crumpling it a little. She turned slowly. "What do you want with me?"

"I told you, just to ask you a few questions."

"Are you the one who had me arrested?"

He looked wary. "You're not under arrest, Miss Hamilton."

"That man, the detective, he said you would try to take me into custody."

His features sharpened. "What detective?"

"The one who called me, from Portersville. He said I shouldn't talk to you."

Kreiger frowned. "Well that was unprofessional, to say the least. I assure you the detective will be reprimanded."

He made an effort to smooth out his features, but even in her distracted state Cathy could tell he was angry, and worried. He said, "I didn't have you arrested, but I *did* arrange for your release.

The reason I did that is because you have some information that's vital to the case I'm working on. As for what the detective told you—it's really better if you don't know any details, but this is a big case, with a lot of prestige, and there's a certain amount of interagency rivalry involved. You can talk to me, or you can talk to him—or you can talk to some stranger in some other precinct or courtroom. But it'll really be easier for everyone concerned if you just cooperate with me, now."

Cathy's eyes were burning with fatigue, her muscles ached, her body quivered with excess adrenaline. The words he had spoken were little more than an annoying background buzz. She said, as evenly as possible, "I'm not under arrest?"

"No."

"Then I don't have to cooperate with anyone, do I?" She started to push past him.

"As far as I'm concerned you can walk out that door right now. Of course, I'll just have to get a warrant and track you down again, and by that time a lot of people may have gotten hurt. I wish you'd reconsider, Miss Hamilton."

Cathy didn't want to reconsider. And it wasn't because of what the detective had said on the phone, or because of the threat of a future warrant, but because she just didn't care. His problems were not her problems; she didn't have time to talk to him now, she didn't *want* to talk to him now.

But six feet away from him she stopped, and looked at the half-crumpled impound slip in her hand in some confusion.

Kreiger was beside her. "It will only take a few minutes," he said gently.

Cathy rubbed her forehead with the back of her wrist. It was hard to think and the road ahead seemed endless, fraught with obstacles. She wasn't sure she could take any more. She didn't know what to do.

Just go, Cathy. Go.

"I'm so tired," she said. Even speaking the words was an effort almost beyond her capabilities.

He touched her arm lightly. "I'll drive you to the impound yard," he said. "We can talk on the way."

After a moment she nodded. She didn't know what else to do.

She thought fatigue would overtake her before she even reached Kreiger's car; she was certain that the moment she sat down the weight of exhaustion would smother her and she would fall asleep. But being in the car, alone with this stranger—a stranger about whom she had been warned—with no sound except the engine and the road noise, had anything but a relaxing effect. Kreiger said nothing, and the silence was suffocating.

He was definitely a policeman, and that knowledge should have reassured her. The dashboard of his car was lined with official equipment: a radio and scanner, a telephone, what appeared to be some kind of miniature computer. But the radio was turned down so low the static was barely a background noise, and the lights from the other electronics gave off an eerie glow. Cathy's nerves were as tight as steel cables as she watched the small town of Hinesville slip away.

Cathy twisted the straps of her purse around her hands. "Why do they keep the cars so far away? Shouldn't it be closer to the police station?"

"Small town police departments don't usually keep their own impound yards. They use private facilities—garages, private lots, whatever they can get cheap."

Nervously, Cathy slipped her hand inside her purse, searching for her keys. *He's a policeman for God's sake, Cathy. Don't do this to yourself.* "I really don't know what I can tell you, Mr. Kreiger. I didn't know any of those people who were—back there. I stopped to make a phone call and all of a sudden this man grabbed me, and then there was shooting . . ."

"The telephone call, Miss Hamilton." His voice was no longer smooth and persuasive but brisk, businesslike. It startled her.

"What? I—I tried to call the hospital. My brother—the line was busy—"

"Not the one you made. The one you took."

Cathy swallowed tightly. Her fingers found the keys and threaded around them briefly for reassurance. Attached to the keychain was a small cylinder encased in leather that purported to be "military tear gas"—similar items were marketed as the perfect self-defense device in drugstores and novelty shops across the country. Cathy had laughed when Jack had given it to her. He had

116

said, "You can't be too careful." She had attached it to her key chain because it made her keys easier to find, and she hadn't thought about it again. Throughout all that had happened tonight, she hadn't thought about it once . . .

Don't be crazy, Cathy. For God's sake, he's a cop.

She said, "I — I don't know what you mean."

The road they were traveling was dark and empty; no streetlights, no buildings, no cars. Farm country. Miles and miles of fields.

He said, "You answered the phone; you took a message. What did the voice on the other end say?"

No, not farm country. Wine country. The fields that stretched as far as the eye could see on either side of the car were actually vineyards.

Her fingers moved over the leather casing of the cylinder. She did not know why she answered as she did, she would never know why. Maybe it was a stranger's voice saying, "Don't talk to him, don't go anywhere with him." Maybe it was Jack's voice saying, "You can't be too careful."

She replied, "He said . . . he said, 'It's off tonight, babe. You've been made.' "

Kreiger said, "You're sure?"

Cathy nodded because a sudden convulsion of her throat made speech impossible. She swallowed, and in a moment managed, "Yes. I'm sure."

He nodded thoughtfully.

Darkness on either side, thick with vines, the

117

endless landscape broken occasionally by a cross-bar support that rose up from the shadows like an executioner's device. The car began to slow, and at first she didn't understand why, then she saw what Kreiger had seen: a dirt road leading off to the right between the unbroken rows of arbors. A service road, traveled by day by tractors and pickup trucks, but by night . . . empty.

He needn't have bothered, Cathy thought. No one would find her . . .

He cut the engine, and the lights. He unfastened his seatbelt and turned toward her. His jacket parted and Cathy saw the gun in his shoulder holster. An evil looking thing, steel and black. *Of course he has a gun. He's a cop.*

She was amazed at how steady her voice sounded as she said, "Are you going to kill me?"

He smiled. It was not a particularly attractive gesture. "No, of course not. I just want you to think, very carefully, about what you really heard on the telephone. Because what you just told me isn't exactly right, is it?"

Her voice was hoarse and didn't sound like her own; neither did the words. "How do you know that? Who are you? What's this all about?"

It couldn't be her, Cathy Hamilton, sitting there so calmly firing questions at this man who was very likely getting ready to kill her, surreptitiously fumbling with the lock on the little canister of tear gas and hoping it didn't explode inside her purse. It couldn't be her, plotting to try to escape from police custody, lying to an officer, staring at an

118

automatic weapon and feeling no fear. Buying time, thinking clearly, doing what she had to do . . .

He said, "I think I've already answered that. Now *I* get to ask the questions."

"I've already told you what I know."

Suddenly his eyes sharpened, though his tone did not. "What have you got in your purse, Cathy? All right, take your hand out, slowly. Bring it up where I can see it."

Cathy took her hand out of her purse, but she didn't do it slowly. He was lunging for her wrist simultaneously as she brought her hand up; the lock came free and she squeezed her eyes shut as she pushed the button.

The sound he made was somewhere between a shout of fury and a gasp of pain. When Cathy opened her eyes she saw him pressed back against the driver's door, clawing at his face, but her own eyes stung with the acrid, ammonia-sharp odor and she knew she had only seconds. *Don't breathe, don't breathe. . . .* She tore at her seat belt, groped for the passenger door release of the automatic locks. His hand struck out blindly and clipped her shoulder, knocking her sideways. *Don't breathe. . . .* She jerked the doorhandle but the door was still locked. She fumbled again for the button, heard a thump inside in the mechanism. He grabbed for her just as she threw the door open, and he caught her shirt at the shoulder, fingernails pinching her flesh. She wrenched herself away from him and felt cloth tear and skin open as she launched herself through the door, landing on her hands and knees in the rocky road. Over her shoulder she saw him lunging toward her, his face red and distorted by the chemical, his movements furious and deadly. She twisted around and kicked the door closed, then scrambled to her feet. She ran.

Instinctively she veered off the road, into the protection of the vineyard and its tall, thick, sheltering vines. Almost immediately she regretted her decision. The lanes of sandy soil between the rows were uneven and the impenetrable density of the vines on either side of her made it impossible to see between them; sound was muffled and all light was cut off. Her sneakers filled with sand and more than once she tripped and fell hard. The gnarled vines and trailing leaves formed silhouettes like a writhing Medusa and she was running through a nightmare, pursued by the sound of her own gasping breath and the plucking skeletal fingers of monsters come to life. Her lungs were burning and she felt exhausted; the panic that rose up inside her was as deadly a threat as the man who might or might not be pursuing her.

Something struck her leg hard, cracking against the bone just below her kneecap. She plunged face forward on the ground, her hands digging for purchase in the soil while agony shot up her leg and spots danced before her eyes. The scream she might have uttered died in her throat as she waited for her pursuer to descend on her.

Except that no one was pursuing her.

The breeze made whispering sounds in the leaves, but nothing moved. And somewhere distant another sound, low familiar, comforting. But no one was chasing her. She had either lost him in the dark or he had been too incapacitated to follow her — or she had been wrong from the beginning and he had never intended to hurt her at all . . .

Don't be a fool, Cathy. Honest cops don't interrogate their witnesses on deserted dirt roads in the middle of the night.

Biting down hard on her lip, she pushed herself into a sitting position, carefully straightening out her leg. It wasn't broken, but when she pushed up her jeans and gingerly touched her shin she could feel a knot already beginning to rise, just below the kneecap. The instrument that had done the damage was within a single sweep of her hands, and she picked it up cautiously. A broken hoe handle. She had tripped over it, flipped it up, and it had struck her in the leg, almost crippling her.

She dropped the hoe handle and used an upright support to pull herself to her feet, cautiously testing her weight on the leg. A bad bruise, nothing more. But she couldn't make herself go any farther; she collapsed against the post, trying to breathe, trying to think, straining to hear above the thunderous sound of her heart.

All right, think. Who was he, what did he want, why had he brought her here? If all he had wanted to do was question her, he could have done that back at the station. If he was the one who had gotten her released, then she had to have been turned over to his custody, and he could have held her as long as he wanted to, until he got the answers he wanted. But he did not want anyone else to hear those answers. So he had told her she was free to go, he had lulled her into a false sense of security so that she would go with him quietly and of her own free will. And when he had her alone . . .

It made no sense. Everyone at the station had seen her leave with him. The paperwork had probably documented his taking over her custody. It would be no secret who was responsible if anything happened to her. But maybe he didn't care. Maybe he was that crazy . . . or that powerful.

Her head ached with trying to reason it out. None of it had ever made sense, not from the beginning, and she would go mad trying to reason it out. She didn't even care *why* anymore. The only thing she cared about was that she was alone in this dark labyrinth of vines and leaves, lost and stranded without a car, without even her purse, and somewhere out there was a madman with a gun.

Her breathing gradually slowed to an almost normal rhythm, but her lungs felt stripped and raw and her leg muscles were like jelly. Her leg hurt abominably. The sweet, fruity quality of the air was cloying, almost nauseating. She had to find a way out of here. Vineyards didn't just tend themselves. Someone owned this one, worked it every day, which meant there was a house somewhere. . . . But Cathy knew that given the size of the standard California vineyard, that house could be ten or twenty miles away in any direction, or there might not be a house at all, because sometimes land was leased, particularly along highways.

Highways. She knew then what that sound was, smooth and comforting in the background. The sound of freeway traffic was as sweet as the murmur of the ocean to her. The interstate. And it wasn't too far away. If she could just find a break in the vines, and follow the sound. . . . The freeway meant civilization. Help. Safety.

She pushed away from the support post, turning toward the sound.

Something grabbed her hair and jerked her sharply backward. Cathy cried out in pain and fear and stumbled for balance. She felt the cold pressure of a steel tube against her temple. Scott Kreiger said softly, "Now we talk."

Alice had once told Dave that the trouble with the world was that the people who ran it had never known desperation. The subject had come up in the midst of an argument about a maid who had stolen a camera — a Polaroid, back when Polaroids were expensive, with a brand new cartridge of film in it. Alice was a social worker, and when she was working full time Dave had insisted she hire someone to come in twice a week to take care of the house; they couldn't really afford it, but tightening up the budget had been easier on Dave than watching Alice work two jobs. She had hired a nice, middle-aged woman, and within a month the camera was gone and so was the woman. Dave was furious, and that was when Alice said she wasn't surprised: she had seen in the woman's eyes that she was familiar with desperation.

Desperation, hell, Dave had shouted, pacing up and down, it wasn't a goddamn loaf of bread, it was a camera, and it wasn't even as though she needed the money. And that was when Alice explained to him that desperation was a relative thing and that, having been touched by it, a person was never the same. Desperation showed you your limits, made you face up to what you were inside and what you were capable of, and for most people that was not a pretty sight. Desperation blurred the lines between right and wrong, desperation made morality a subjective thing, desperation stripped away the trappings of civilization, however briefly, and returned the human animal to the jungle. Some people, no matter how well they might pretend otherwise, never quite escaped the shadow of that jungle. Some people found the truth about what they were capable of far too easy to live with, and that was basically the only difference between a cop and a woman who stole a camera she didn't need.

She refused to let him press charges, and that infuriated Dave further; they argued about that longer and harder than they had ever argued about anything before, mostly because Dave knew she was right. And he had thought about desperation, and the things it did to you—sometimes subtle, sometimes immutable—a great deal since then.

He thought about desperation now. And he thought about Cathy Hamilton, who, he knew with an almost clairvoyant certainty, had never been touched by the cold breath of terror before in her life. Cathy Hamilton, small-town school teacher, threatened with the loss of someone she loved, suddenly confronted with violence and death, betrayed by the very system she, as a product of middle America, had been taught to trust. What was she capable of? Did she know her limits yet?

She hadn't believed him about Kreiger. She had barely even listened to him. She hadn't cared about Kreiger, and Dave couldn't blame her. Her world had been brutally invaded and turned upside down, and she couldn't be expected to trust the voice of a stranger over the telephone.

If Kreiger had her, she was beyond help. But if anything he had said had gotten through to her, if some twist of fate had allowed her to elude Kreiger . . . *Cathy Hamilton,* he thought, his fingers gripping the wheel in tightening frustration, *tell me who you are, how you think. I need to know. Where will you go, what will you do, who are you going to turn to when you're in trouble?*

The car phone had been Toby's idea. For Dave's part, the police radio had served communication needs for almost half a century, and he saw no need to augment it now, but he had stood back and listened in silent amusement while Toby argued the usefulness of car phones for undercover work and hostage situations. Toby was eloquent, and eventually the department had agreed to equip each detective team with a car phone; the county paid three-quarters, the rest was personal expense. So far, the only time Dave had used the car phone was to call Toby when he was running late. Tonight, however, it was finally going to live up to the potential Toby had envisioned for it. Tonight, as far as Dave was concerned, the phone might very well mean the difference between life and death.

He picked it up and, briefly consulting the scrap of paper in his pocket, punched out a series of numbers. The wait for the switches and relays seemed interminable. Then a woman's voice, sharp with strain, answered.

"Miss Brian? This is Detective Jenks again."

"Oh, God. Cathy—where is she? Is she okay?"

I hate this, Dave thought. "I was hoping you'd heard from her."

"I—I did, but just for a minute and she sounded terrible. She said she was in trouble, that she didn't know where she was and she was scared—then she hung up before I could ask her . . ."

His only hope faded. If Cathy had remained in custody, she would have called her friend for help. Kreiger had gotten to her.

"What time was that?"

126

"About three, a little after."

About the same time, Dave reflected, that the anonymous call about Frazier had come in. It had been Cathy making that report, Dave was sure of it. Frazier had frightened her, she'd run from him, then she'd stopped — as terrified as she must have been, she'd stopped at the nearest phone booth and reported a man injured, because that's what good citizens did. Dave tried to imagine the kind of courage it must have taken for her to do that. After being caught in the middle of a gun battle and sprayed with blood, after being chased and trapped and threatened with a gun and being forced to hit a man with her car in order to escape . . . to stop and make a phone call to report the accident, to expose herself again to the terrors that awaited her in the dark, was an act of bravery that Dave, who had seen his share of valor under fire, had to admire.

"Detective? Detective, please, won't you tell me what's going on?"

He focused his attention with an effort. "Miss Brian — you're Cathy's roommate, right?"

"No, just her friend. We both teach at the same school. This is her brother's house. She — he's divorced, his wife just walked out on him and the kids a few years back, nobody even knows where she is now, not even her own mother, and Cathy — well, Cathy just kind of stepped in to help out."

Dave had looked up Lynn Haven in the atlas back at the station. Population three thousand, not counting the college students. Thirty miles from the coast, far enough from the ocean to avoid the tourists but close enough to smell the sea on rainy days. Apartments would be scarce, and geared toward the college population. He pictured Cathy's house—her brother's house—in a quiet, older neighborhood, shaded by trees and planted with flower beds.

He said, "No, I can't tell you what's going on. Only that I'm trying to help your friend, and anything you can do to help me will be appreciated."

There was a hesitation, filled with uncertainty. "I—I don't know what I can do."

"The hospital. Have you heard anything about her brother? I'm on my way to her now and I'd like to bring her some good news."

"There isn't any, I'm afraid. He's in intensive care and hasn't regained consciousness."

"Children?"

"They weren't hurt. How did you know about the children?"

"I talked to Cathy, for just a minute. She said she was their only relative."

"They have a grandmother. She's flying out but it'll be sometime tomorrow before she gets here. Oh, God, it should only be a five hour drive from here."

He heard the woman's voice start to break, and he overrode her firmly, "Is there anyone else Cathy might call, besides you, for help?"

The muffled sound on the other end of the phone might have been a sniffle or a sob. It was a moment before she replied, in a slightly calmer tone, "She has friends, of course, but she'd call me first. I mean under ordinary circumstances she'd call Jack. They're twins, did you know that? Very close. He's a teacher, too—a professor, actually, at the college. Literature. Cathy teaches music, she's really incredibly talented. Everyone says she should be with a big orchestra somewhere, and I guess the only reason she ended up in a place like this was because of Jack. Words and music, that's what she told me Jack used to say. That's how close they are, like words and music. I'm babbling. You don't want—"

"Yes," he said quickly. "Yes, that's exactly what I want. Anything you can tell me about her, everything you can think of. I've got to try to find her and time is running out. The only clues I have are the ones you can give me. So talk to me, Miss Brian. Please."

Hesitantly, stumbling at first and then with more confidence, Ellen began. "I—the orchestra. She helped start a community orchestra, and tonight was the debut. It was quite a success. It was her birthday, too, hers and Jack's, and we had a little party. Jack never would have missed it if . . ."

She talked, and Dave listened. He listened as though his life depended on learning everything he could about Cathy Hamilton. He knew that Cathy's already did.

Kreiger said, "You were right. I am going

129

to have to kill you. I probably wouldn't have, before, but now that you and Detective Jenks are such good friends—"

Cathy gasped, "I don't know who you're talking about! I never—never even met the man!" The barrel of the gun pressed so hard into her temple that she could imagine it boring a perfect hole through the fragile barrier of skin and cartilage, stabbing into her brain. She concentrated all her energy on trying to inch her temple away from the pressure of that steel tube, but he wound his hand tighter in her hair, bringing stinging tears into her eyes.

"You see," Kreiger went on calmly, "only one person is allowed to know what you're about to tell me. And you are going to tell me, aren't you?"

Cathy whispered, "Yes." It seemed to her that the pressure of the gun on her temple eased a bit then, and she repeated gratefully, "Yes!"

He relaxed his grip on her hair slightly and she gasped out loud with the sudden lessening of pain. "That's good. Maybe I won't have to kill you, after all. That is if you tell me the truth this time. I don't have time to waste on you, lady, and if you start jerking me around . . ."

"I won't. Don't hurt me, please. I'll tell you. I'll tell you whatever you want to know."

He released her hair, but not the pressure of the gun against her temple. It was instinct, combined with the throbbing pain in her leg and the very real weakness of her muscles, that caused Cathy to sink to the ground. Her collapse seemed to startle him, and it gave Cathy the precious few moments she needed. He bent down angrily to jerk her back to her feet and Cathy swung around, wielding the hoe handle with both hands.

If she had swung a half-second earlier or a half-second later the handle would have struck his hard-muscled shoulder, hurting him and perhaps casting him momentarily off balance, but doing no measurable damage. But the luck of the blind and the innocent was on her side, and she swung her weapon just as he bent into its path. The solid oak handle connected with the side of his neck with a force that knocked him to his knees, and sent a shock wave of pain up Cathy's arm that almost caused her to lose her grip on the weapon.

He grabbed at his neck, his face contorted with pain, yet still turned toward her. Sobbing for breath, Cathy stumbled to her feet and felt him grab her ankle. Sheer terror sent a new surge of strength through her and it was again with instinct more than forethought that she swung again, like she would swing at a rabid animal that was charging her—hard, with the power born of the desperate instinct for self-defense. She screamed at the sound the handle made when it struck the side of his head and at the sight of blood bursting on his face. He fell forward into the dirt.

Gasping, shaking with exertion and horror and disbelief, Cathy took a staggering step backward. She looked at the hoe handle in her hand and saw something dark and wet shine dully on its end. She dropped it as though it were alive. Nausea swam and she brought the back of her hand to her mouth, certain for a moment that she was going to be sick. She took another uncertain step backward.

And then the dull glint of something metal caught her eye. Lying half-hidden in the shadow of vines, perhaps a foot from Kreiger's outstretched fingers, . . . was his gun.

Cathy wanted to run. She wanted to turn her back on the inert, bleeding form of the man who had as much as promised to kill her, she wanted to forget she had ever seen that weapon, she wanted to just turn and run as far as she could and as fast as she could, to get away from here before he regained consciousness. Before *he* saw the gun . . .

Pressing her fingertips hard against her lips as though to physically hold back the sobs that wanted to break through, Cathy edged around Kreiger's crumpled body, staying as far as possible away from feet that could suddenly kick out, hands that could grab with snake-like swiftness. She glanced at the gun. She glanced at Kreiger. There was no way she could reach it without leaning over him. She knelt down, holding her breath, stretching out her arm.

He moaned.

Cathy snatched up the gun and backed away, dragging in breaths that sounded like sobs, holding the weapon in both hands, pointed at him. She even put her finger on the trigger. He made another sound and stirred, and Cathy tripped over an uneven hillock, almost falling. Then she turned, and ran.

She ran, stumbling, sobbing, through the night. She didn't know where she was going, she didn't know what she was going to do when she got there. She didn't know who to turn to, who to trust. The only thing she knew was that she had to keep running.

Jack, she thought, *I don't know what to do . . . help me . . . tell me what to do . . .*

But just like every other time she had mentally turned to Jack during this hellish night, there was nothing but silence in reply.

Chapter Nine

Cathy felt neither joy nor relief when the free-way came into sight. She wasn't sure how she had reached it or how long it had taken her, nor did she care. She couldn't remember why it had ever been important to reach the freeway in the first place.

Dazed and numbed, bleeding from a dozen small cuts and favoring her injured right leg, Cathy started down the embankment that sloped toward the underpass. The grass was wet with dew and she slipped, half-sliding, half-stumbling down the hill toward the blacktop. She landed in a gully beside the emergency lane. When she stood up the backdraft from a tractor-trailer roared in her ears and almost knocked her off balance.

She started toward the asphalt, but then stopped. Anyone could see her there. A lone woman on the side of the freeway in the middle of the night — she would be perfect prey. Kreiger's pistol was tucked into the waistband of her jeans, where it was more of a discomfort than a reassurance—all it meant was that if someone tried to attack her he would have easy access to a weapon to do the job right. She thought dully, *It doesn't matter. I don't care.* And she didn't. But she stayed to the shadows of the gully as she continued her trudge north, paralleling the flow of traffic.

All her life she had depended on Jack, and she had done so without question or hesitation, as naturally as breathing. He had always been there, again without question or hesitation, to provide whatever it was she needed. Never had he asked anything of her. Never had he needed her . . . until now. And she had failed him.

Her brother was dead, and she was empty inside.

For all of her life there had been two parts of her: the part that was Cathy, and the part that was Jack, separate but the same. No one who wasn't a twin would understand. No matter where she was or what she was doing, a small part of him was always with her. She was never alone. But now, when she reached inside herself for that reassuring presence, she felt . . . nothing. Jack was gone.

Up ahead was an exit sign, and she struggled toward it. Her feet were soaked with dew and tingling with fatigue, her leg muscles ached all the way into her hips. Her clothes were damp with perspiration and she was chilled to the bone, and she wondered, briefly and without much energy, why she even bothered to keep walking, why she didn't just let her legs collapse and sit down on the side of the road and wait until someone found her. But the children — she had to get to the children, Jack would want her to take care of the children.

And besides, she had been moving so long she wasn't sure she knew how to stop.

At first she thought it was a mirage. The lights were too bright, the colors too intense to be real, and as she stared at it the building, with its red tile roof and bright windows, actually seemed to shimmer and fade. But Cathy blinked, and it *was* real. A truck stop, not very big and not very busy, but real, a bright oasis against the endless night. She started toward it.

She felt as though she were swimming under water, pushing up toward the surface. With every step she shed another layer of the numbing shock that had enfolded her, and reality became a little clearer. At first she was not sure why it was so important to reach the building, but by the time she passed out of the shadows of the big rig that was parked in front, she knew. Civilization. Sanity. Refuge. They all waited for her inside the restaurant.

She pushed open the door, and her courage, her resolve, the strength that had carried her this far, all deserted her. She just stood there, dazzled by the brightness, the warmth, the normalcy of it all.

It smelled like bacon and home fries and maple syrup. Willie Nelson was on the juke box. There was a curly-haired waitress in a pink uniform with a stain on the pocket, and a man at the grill wearing a white paper hat. A big, beefy man in a red tee shirt sat at the counter, a man and a woman shared a booth. They all turned to look at Cathy when she came in.

Cathy wanted to burst into tears of exhaustion and relief. No one here had ever chased anyone else with a gun. No one here knew about death in the night and cryptic phone messages and policemen who turned their weapons on bystanders. Here were nothing but ordinary people living ordinary lives. Here she was safe.

It took her a long time to realize they were staring at her. She did not need the glimpse she caught of her reflection in the window to tell her why. Her nightshirt was torn, her jeans muddy and studded with small thorns and burrs. Her hair was tangled and dusted with leaves, and there were scratches on her face and arms. She parted her lips to say something—and suddenly realized she didn't know what to say. Could she plead for help, tell them someone was trying to kill her? Even if they believed her they would only call the police, and that was the last thing she wanted. What she wanted was to leave this place, to put it all far, far behind her, but she didn't have a car. She didn't even have her purse. Money, identification, keys, all of it was back in a car at the end of a dirt road in the middle of a vineyard somewhere.

The big man, a half-eaten hamburger dripping ketchup down his arm, chewed slowly as he watched her. The waitress, mopping the counter, never took her eyes off her. The couple in the booth glanced uneasily at one another. The man in the paper hat scowled, coming toward her.

She had to think. It had seemed so simple at first, a single, clearly directed goal. Lights. Safety. Help. But now she had to think. She didn't know what to do anymore. She was so tired.

She saw the sign indicating restrooms toward her right. If she had had to walk past all those people she might not have made it. But she simply turned her back on them and went into the ladies' room. There she felt almost safe.

She braced her arms on the sink, dropping her head, breathing deeply to try to clear the fog from her brain. When she lifted her face the reflection in the mirror startled her, and she almost did not recognize it as her own. Her face was paper white, her eyes so sunken and dark shadowed they looked like a mask. Two bright red scratches scored her right cheek and blood was smeared in the area between them. Her hair was wild and dusted with debris. And she could see very clearly beneath her nightshirt what everyone had been staring at — the outline of the gun.

There was a moment — a truly frightening moment — when she felt the hysterical urge to laugh, and she knew if she gave in to that impulse she would be abandoning reason forever. So she closed her eyes and breathed deeply through her nostrils, and when she opened her eyes again she made herself lift her shirt and grasp the gun by the handle.

She hated the feel of it. She could not believe she had stuffed it inside her jeans like that, like a street crook or an old-time outlaw . . . like she knew what she was doing. It had left a red imprint, barrel and handle, against the soft flesh of her abdomen, and the steel was sticky and warm. She held it delicately with two fingers, and her strongest impulse was to drop it into the trashcan. She didn't know what stopped her.

She put the gun on the small shelf above the sink and turned on the faucets. The water ran for a long time before she bent, slowly and stiffly, to wash her face. She needed help. She had to get her car back. Her purse, her money . . .

She heard the swinging door open and she turned away quickly, tucking the gun back into her waistband. Her heart was beating hard, though not from fear of who might come through the door. It was simply that instinct had returned, and the same terror that had pursued her on phantom wings throughout the night. She couldn't afford to relax. She wasn't safe, not yet. She had to *think* . . .

The waitress came around the corner. She watched with frank curiosity and no small amount of suspicion as Cathy pulled a paper towel from the dispenser and blotted her face, then her hands.

The waitress said, "Sal—he's the night cook—he sent me in here to get rid of you. Says we don't need no trouble here."

Cathy dropped the paper towel into the trash and pulled another one from the dispenser, using it to dry her hands. She moved slowly, buying time, trying to think what to do. The most important thing was money. How could she do anything without money? Her checkbook, her credit cards, all those little lifelines, such an integral part of everyday life that she had never had the opportunity to even imagine being without them—suddenly they were gone, and she was stranded. She could feel panic rising up in her chest and she fought it back with all her might.

She dropped the towel into the trash and half-turned back to the sink, slipping her fingers into her jeans pocket in hope of coming up with a bill she had stashed there long ago and forgotten, or even a handful of change. Her fingers touched a folded paper instead.

She turned back to the waitress, raising her

eyes slowly, speaking with an effort and as though from a great distance. "I—need to make a phone call."

The waitress hitched one shoulder back toward the door. "Pay phone's in the hall, right when you go out."

Cathy's voice was hollow. "I don't have any money."

The other woman eyed her skeptically. "Some man do this to you?" she demanded.

After a moment, Cathy nodded.

The waitress's eyes narrowed. "Your old man?"

Some instinct urged Cathy to nod again. "Yes," she whispered. "I need—I need to call someone to come get me."

An expression like disgust crossed the other woman's face, and Cathy thought she had made a mistake. But then she muttered, "Shit. I guess I've been there before."

She dug into her uniform pocket and produced a quarter. "Make your phone call, honey. But if you call that man of yours and he shows up here tearing up the place, it's *my* ass, you got that?"

Cathy's hand closed around the quarter, but her throat was so swollen with gratitude and relief she almost couldn't get the words out. "Thank you."

She followed the waitress out of the restroom, and stopped at the pay phone in the corridor as the other woman went back up to the grill. She took the paper out of her pocket. Her hand shook, making it hard to read the numbers. She concentrated, dialing carefully.

The phone rang. From somewhere very far away, a man's voice answered.

It was at that moment that the final muffling layer of shock dropped away. She began to shake, all over. Tears coursed down her cheeks. She gripped the receiver hard and tried to speak.

"Hello," he said again. "Who is this? Talk to me."

"Please," she managed brokenly at last. Her voice sounded very tiny, and lost. "Help me . . ."

Chapter Ten

By the time Dave finished talking to Ellen Brian, he knew Cathy Hamilton didn't have much of a chance. The odds were against the average man in a contest of skills and wit with Kreiger, but for a woman like Cathy . . . if Dave found her, and that was a big if, it would probably be too late. He knew Kreiger had taken her, and he knew Kreiger wasn't going to leave any loose ends once he got the information he needed from her. The only thing Dave didn't know was why he continued to drive north, when there was almost no possibility Cathy Hamilton was still alive and an even smaller chance that he would stumble on her in the dark.

All he could do was follow her, start at the Hinesville station and try to pick up clues along the way as to where Kreiger might have taken her. He guessed it wouldn't have been far, for Kreiger had struck him as a man who didn't have a great deal of time to waste. And there was always the chance that something in his behavior, or Cathy's, had alerted the Hinesville police and they had gone after him. Or perhaps they had refused to release Cathy to him. A chance, but it was almost infinitesimal.

Then why was he taking the Hinesville exit? Why was he risking his job, disobeying a direct order, and taking a chance on bringing embarrassment to the department—not to mention embroiling himself and his chief in an unpleasant confrontation with the FBI—for the sake of a woman he didn't know and who was completely out of his jurisdiction? There were moments after he hung up the phone with Ellen, listening to the sound of his tires against the highway and watching the miles flash by, when he didn't know. But there were other times when the answer was so simple it practically rang in his head.

There were too many accidents in the world, too many mistakes, too many innocent bystanders. Too many bad things happened to people who didn't deserve them, and Dave had stood by and watched it happen for too long. He couldn't take back the bullet that had ripped apart Toby's spine, any more than, five years ago, he had been able to fight back the cancer that had eaten away Alice's life. But Cathy Hamilton . . . maybe he could do something about her. Maybe the madness could stop here.

And then she called him. He let his foot ease off the accelerator when he heard her voice; the relief that went through him was so acute that he couldn't focus on anything else. She had survived. Somehow she had made it this far, she had beaten the odds, and Dave knew without a doubt why he had come after her. He also knew nothing was going to stop him now.

He said, trying not to let the emotion show in his voice, "Cathy. Are you all right?"

No answer. Perhaps she nodded, but the background noise was muffled so perhaps she put her hand over the receiver. She was crying.

"Are you alone?" Still, he kept the urgency out of his voice. If she had only managed to sneak away from Kreiger for a moment, or worse, if he were standing there with her, holding a gun to her head while she lured Dave into a trap . . .

She said, "Yes." Her voice was thin, and strained with the effort not to let the tears show. "I mean, there are people here—a few . . . my car, my purse . . ."

"It's okay." Quietly, calmly. "Where are you?"

"A truck stop. I don't have any money. I left my purse in his car, and the police impounded my car . . . My keys, my credit cards—"

"Do you know where this truck stop is?"

A pause, interrupted only by a muffled sound that might have been another choked-back sob. But her voice was stronger when she answered. "It's—it's called Harvey's. It's off I-5, going north. The exit sign said Mill Brook Road."

Dave said, "Stay there. I'm ten minutes away."

He stepped on the brakes, hard, and spun into

145

a U-turn, heading back toward the freeway.

Cathy wasn't sure how long it was after she hung up the phone that she began to wonder if she had made a mistake. Dave Jenks had said he was a police officer—but so had Kreiger. She had seen Kreiger's badge, she had been inside his car, complete with all its official law enforcement equipment, and he had tried to kill her. She hadn't so much as seen Dave Jenks' face. And even if Dave Jenks was with the Portersville Police Department, she couldn't be sure that the man on the other end of the phone *was* Dave Jenks. If there was one thing she had learned tonight, it was that nothing was necessarily as it appeared to be; perhaps she had been a fool to tell a stranger on the telephone where she was.

Except—his voice. Twice she had heard his voice now, and it was an island of peace in the midst of a raging storm. Kind, calm, strong. It was the kind of voice that made her want to close her eyes and forget to be afraid, to just relax and let him take control. It was a voice she wanted to trust.

Please, she thought. *Please don't let it be a mistake.* She had a feeling she did not have too many more mistakes left.

The waitress and the man at the grill were arguing when Cathy came out, and she knew it was about her. She didn't need the cook's glare to remind her that she wasn't wanted here. When the waitress set a cup of coffee on the counter and invited, somewhat defiantly, a little too loudly, "Sit down here, honey, and have some of this," Cathy would have preferred not to have the attention drawn to her.

She hesitated, and said to the waitress in a muffled tone, "I don't have any—"

"My treat," the other woman replied, and there was no mistaking the defiance in the glance she tossed over her shoulder to the cook. "You want a piece of pie?"

There was nothing Cathy could do then but sit down on one of the high stools. "No," she said, "thank you." She wrapped her hands around the coffee cup and wished she had waited outside. She should have taken comfort in the presence of other people, in the lights, in the familiar sounds and smells of the place. But she felt exposed in the same way she had felt exposed in the phone booth. Too many lights, too many windows. Too many people staring at her.

She tried to take a sip of coffee, but her shaking hands sloshed a good portion of it onto the saucer before she had lifted it more than a few inches. Ten minutes, he had said. What if ten minutes passed and no one came? Twenty minutes? How long could she wait here? She should call Ellen. She should call the hospital—but her weary mind shrank away from the thought of doing so. She knew what they would tell her. She knew what they would tell her and she couldn't stand it now. No, she should call Ellen and tell her where she was, just in case . . . but

Ellen seemed far, far away from the world of insanity into which she had been plunged, hardly real, completely useless to Cathy in this time and place. Besides, she didn't have a quarter, and she refused to ask the waitress for anything else.

The big man in the red tee shirt was staring at her boldly, with the same sort of absent interest he might give a television set or a magazine cover, as though he had every right to do so. It made Cathy's skin crawl, and when at last she slid an uneasy glance toward him he didn't even have the shame to avert his gaze. Instead he said, around a mouthful of French fries, "You got troubles, little lady?"

Cathy picked up her coffee cup, with both hands this time, hoping if she didn't answer he would lose interest. Every nerve in her body tightened for flight.

He said, "Because me and my rig, we're heading up to Canada." His voice was low, and greasy like his skin, "and you ain't got nothing I can't cure, believe me. Now if you was to take a mind to come along . . ."

Cathy slid off the stool and moved toward the door, her muscles tensing against the expectation of a harsh hand grabbing her shoulder or a voice calling her back. But when she caught a reflection of the interior of the room in the glass door, the big man had turned back to his hamburger, and she saw the waitress shrug and start wiping off menus. Only the cook continued to glare at her, and it was clear he was glad to see her go.

The night air felt warm on her skin after the air-conditioned restaurant. The parking lot lights formed on the asphalt pools of pinkish illumination that faded into shadow pits all around. In the distance, the freeway murmured its soothing ocean sounds. She realized the moment she stepped outside how stupid it was of her to leave the security of lights and other people. What if the truck driver came after her? She couldn't fight him off in a dark parking lot, and she couldn't expect help from any of the men inside. On the other hand, maybe she should have accepted his offer of a ride. That might well have been her only guarantee of safe passage, for at least she knew that *he* had no connection to the events in Portersville, California.

She stood close to the building, taking protection from the light that flooded through the doors and windows, and knowing that by doing so she risked being seen before she could see, should anyone come for her. She could only hope that it would be a risk worth taking, because she actually heard the car exit the freeway and enter the parking lot from the back side before she saw it. It could have been anyone, of course: a late-night traveler or early-morning commuter stopping for breakfast, a delivery van or milk truck—but it wasn't. It was a blue sedan, nondescript in its ordinariness, and yet somehow vaguely familiar to Cathy. It moved slowly round the building, and when the driver saw Cathy he pulled up to the curb, rather than turning toward the parking lot. It was him. He had come for her.

Her heart was pounding hard and her nails dug into her palms as she tried to remain calm, to breathe deeply. She wanted to move toward him, but her legs had no strength. She wanted to burst into tears but she didn't dare. And then he opened the door to get out, and in the car's interior light she saw him.

It was the man in the red fishing hat.

There was a moment when her consciousness seemed to stop and the entire world was caught between one breath and another, like a strobe light frozen in time. There was a man in a navy nylon windbreaker and a red fishing hat, ordinary face, quiet eyes, watching her as he got out of his car. And there was that same man, his face contorted with rage, his feet planted in a gunman's stance and his hands gripping a revolver that was pointed at her.

She had just used up the last of her mistakes.

He said, "Hello, Cathy."

She took one stumbling step backward. She saw his face start to change. He shouted, "Cathy!" as she broke into a run.

Her heart was bursting in her chest as she ran toward the back of the building, away from the lights, and she could hear his footsteps pounding on the pavement behind her. She thought, *I can't do this anymore. I can't!* Her bruised leg stabbed with pain every time she put her foot down and her stiff muscles responded sluggishly; panic tightened her chest and she couldn't breathe. His legs were longer than hers and his footsteps were getting closer. He shouted her name again, and it sounded as though he was right next to her ear. The gun in her waistband stabbed against her hip bone, causing her to stumble. She couldn't keep on running forever, she couldn't run another minute.

Before her there was a set of dumpsters and a chain-link fence. Inky lakes of shadow spread out toward the lights that came from the windows at the side of the building. Her eyes darted toward the fence, but she couldn't climb it; toward the dumpsters, but she couldn't hide there. The building—she'd never make it. There was no place left to run. And she was too tired to run anymore anyway; he was gaining on her.

Suddenly the panic transformed itself into anger. She shouldn't *have* to run. She hadn't done anything wrong and it wasn't fair. She was tired and scared and hurt and it *wasn't fair.*

And with that surge of anger and despair welling up inside her and the sound of his footsteps pounding down on her, Cathy stopped, tugging the gun from her jeans, and she whirled.

"Stop it!" she screamed. She gripped the gun with both hands and held it steady on him. "Just—stop it!"

He stopped, his hands raised to his waist in an instinctive gesture of self-defense—or surrender— and with startlement registering on his face.

Cathy felt a rush of power that was almost dizzying, and her hands tightened on the butt of the gun. She wasn't helpless! For the first time since the whole nightmare began, she was not the victim. She could make it stop.

He said, quietly, a little out of breath, "Cathy . . ."

"Shut up!" she screamed at him. "Don't call me that!" Her finger sought the trigger and his eyes watched her movement. Pleasure swelled, fierce and intense, at the power she commanded through so small a thing as the placement of her finger. She focused on him in the dim light, expecting—hoping—to see fear in his eyes, and a little disappointed when she did not.

He was slowly getting his breath back, a man who was no more used to sudden bursts of speed—or terror—than she was. "Cathy," he insisted quietly, "what happened? Why are you doing this?" His voice, so calm, so soothing, so in control. The same voice she had heard before, urging from her now as it had then her most precious possession—her trust.

The sound of his voice confused her. She flexed her fingers on the gun for reassurance. "Who are you?" she demanded hoarsely. "How did you find me?"

His brows drew together a little in disturbance. "You know who I am. You called me."

"Don't lie to me!"

"I'm Dave Jenks. You called me for help."

"You tried to kill me! I saw you! You would

152

have shot me back at the mini-mart if you could have, and later, when I called for help from the shopping center *you* came instead, looking for me with your gun! Did you think I wouldn't remember? Did you think I wouldn't recognize you?"

Dave's face cleared as it suddenly all came together for him. "For God's sake, Cathy, I'm a cop! Of course I have a gun. That was my partner who got killed back there—"

"And Kreiger? Is he your partner too?"

He said urgently. "Where is he? How did you get away from him? Did he—"

"Shut up! I don't have to tell you anything!"

As he blurted out his barrage of questions he had taken a step toward her. Cathy jerked the pistol at him and he stopped.

Keeping his hands visible, palms up, near his waist, Dave said, "Listen to me. I'm on your side. There's a lot you don't know, a lot you don't understand—a lot *I* don't understand, but I'm not going to explain it to you here in this parking lot, at gunpoint. I want to help you, but you've got to trust me."

Her head was spinning, aching, she couldn't think. She didn't *want* to think, she didn't want to understand. She just wanted it all to go away.

"Come on, Cathy . . ."

He moved toward her again, and she jerked the gun, her finger settling soundly on the trigger. Again he stopped, but it seemed more of a polite gesture than a worried one.

"What are you going to do?" he asked. "Shoot me? And then what? You're in trouble, Cathy, more than you know, and if Kreiger is still at large, and I think he is, it's only going to get worse. I'm the only friend you've got right now, so for God's sake put down the gun and let's talk."

"No."

Her voice was hoarse, broken on even that one syllable. She gripped the gun as if it were a lifeline, but Dave could see uncertainty in her eyes; the slightest hint of a waver. She was a woman battered by exhaustion and terror, hovering on the ragged edge of collapse, and Dave knew better than to bet his life on which way she would turn if pushed too far. But that was exactly what he had to do.

He knew Cathy Hamilton. Over the past few hours he had made it his mission to know her as well as anyone had ever known her, and that meant more than just assimilating a collection of facts. She had become real to him; pieces of a puzzle he had put together to form a living, breathing being, with feelings and motives, actions and reactions he knew as well as he knew his own. But now was the time he would find out whether he had put the pieces together right, and he knew he would only get one chance.

He said, "I know you're tired. I know you're not thinking clearly. If you were, you'd realize that if I really wanted to hurt you I would have come after you with a gun just now. I didn't have to let you pull a weapon on me."

That made sense to Cathy. She *was* tired. She couldn't think of an argument for what he said. Or maybe it was just that she wanted to believe him, just that his voice was so convincing . . .

She realized the tip of the gun had dropped down and she moved it level again with a snap. Her arms ached with the effort of holding it. She said sharply, "No. You want to take me back with you. I'm not going back, I can't go back—"

"I'm not going to take you back," he assured her. Soothing, gentle, sincere. So easy to believe. "I know you have to get to Jack. I only want to make sure you get there safely."

Jack. It was as though a door had been opened with that single word, opened just a crack, but it was enough to allow the emotions to come seeping through, and the memories, and the needs. They pushed the door wider, and wider . . . she tried to fight the shaking in her voice, she tried to keep the gun steady. She tried to stay strong, but it hardly seemed worth the effort.

"Jack," she whispered, trying not to make it a plea. "What—do you know about him? Is he . . ." She couldn't say it.

"He's in bad shape, Cathy," Dave told her soberly. "I wish I had better news, but I don't. He's in intensive care, and unconscious, and that's all I know. But he's alive."

Alive. It wasn't possible. She knew it wasn't

155

possible, with all the horrors that had overtaken her, that she should be spared that, the grandest horror of all. Yet when Dave Jenks said that her brother was alive, she believed him. She *wanted* to believe him, so desperately . . .

"Don't lie to me!" she screamed at him. The cry was ripped out of her throat, almost as though it had come from a source other than herself, and it hurt. "I'll kill you, I swear to God I will! I'm not having any more lies, I'm not going to be tricked again, I'm not!"

"Cathy, for God's sake—"

A sudden sound startled her—somewhere between a creak and a crash—and a wedge of light burst over her, pinning her in its glare. She blinked and instinctively averted her face, and she knew in that second, or in any that followed, Dave Jenks could have disarmed her without so much as a whimper of resistance on her part. But he didn't. It could have been that he too, was startled; it could have been that there wasn't time, or he was afraid to take the chance—but Cathy knew on some deep instinctual level even then that it was none of those things. He simply didn't do it.

It was the cook who walked into the square of light cast by the open door, a barrel of trash in his hands. He stopped with an almost comical abruptness, staring at them; he exclaimed, "What the hell?" and then he dropped—or perhaps he threw—the trash barrel and ran back inside, slamming the door hard behind him.

Cathy stood there shaking in the dark, and after a moment Dave spoke again, quietly, as though nothing had happened to interrupt them. "If I could think of a lie that would get you to trust me, I'd tell it. But I can't. I can only tell you what I know and none of it looks good for you, Cathy."

"Please." Her voice was small, tired, straining to remain steady. "Please just let me go. Just go away and let me go."

"Yes," he said slowly, "I could do that. But I came all the way from Portersville so that I wouldn't have to have you on my conscience, and if I let you walk away now you'll be dead before another night falls." He glanced toward the back door, now just another shadow among shadows. "He's calling the police, you know. I don't think you want that. I'm out of my jurisdiction, there nothing I can do officially to help you. I'm risking my job just by coming this far, and if there's a police report my ass'll end up in jail just as quick as yours. Only I'd probably get out in an hour or two. I don't know about you. What's it going to be, Cathy?"

No, she couldn't let the police find her. She had to run. She had to get out of here, she had to find some place safe to hide, and think. . . . But she was so tired, and there didn't seem to be a safe place in the world.

The small muscles in her wrists strained and trembled to keep the gun held steady. And what she said next was not what she had intended to say at all. "How—do you know about Jack?"

His voice was gentle as he took a step toward her. "Words and music, isn't that what he used to say?"

"Stop it, please, don't come any closer!"

"What do you think he would say now?"

He was still coming toward her, and she couldn't make him stop. "Don't, please! Don't make me—"

He was half-a-dozen steps from her now. He said, "You're not going to shoot me, Cathy. Just put the gun down."

She didn't want to. She didn't intend to. But the gun was so heavy and her arms were so tired, and she was tired of running, and he was right. She couldn't pull the trigger. Tears flooded her throat, brimming over into her eyes as she let her arms drop. "I don't know," she whispered. "I don't know what Jack would say . . ."

He was beside her in an instant, and it seemed then the most natural thing in the world that his arms should go around her, his strong hand pressing her head to his shoulder as the tears overflowed. "It's okay, honey," he said. He was breathing deeply, as though with a deliberate effort to calm himself. "It's going to be okay."

She cried, though she hated herself for crying, because she was tired and she couldn't stop herself, and because he was strong. And it was good, for just a short time, to lean on someone and to believe she could trust him. But she fought it, she struggled to maintain control, and in a few minutes she managed to stop the tears.

Gently, Dave removed the gun from her hand. He glanced at it, and then at her. He flipped a small button, which, Cathy realized after a moment, released the safety catch.

"The first thing we're going to do," he said, "is teach you how to use this thing." He snapped the safety back on and zipped the gun in the front pocket of his windbreaker. "But right now we'd better get out of here. I figure the police are about five minutes away."

He touched her shoulder and his urgency communicated itself through his fingertips more clearly than words could have done. She hurried with him around the side of the building.

And even though she knew it was foolish, even though all the wisdom she had earned tonight warned her otherwise, Cathy *did* believe suddenly that everything would be all right. She wasn't alone anymore. She wasn't helpless anymore. Dave Jenks was on her side. He would take care of her.

They moved quickly through the bright light at the front of the building toward his waiting car, and Cathy tried not to look at the windows, where she knew people were staring out at them. Instead she cast a quick glance at Dave. "Where are we—"

The explosion of a gunshot tore through the night, and Cathy hit the asphalt hard as the impact of Dave's body flung her forward.

Chapter Eleven

It took only seconds. In Cathy's mind a voice was screaming, *No, it can't be, this can't be happening, don't let this be happening!* as her hands scraped the asphalt. But before her knees struck the ground someone grabbed her shirt at the back of the neck and jerked her to her feet, launching her toward the car.

"Keep your head down!" Dave Jenks shouted. "Run!"

He had left the driver's-side door open when he had been forced to chase her, and Cathy scrambled inside. He was right beside her, pushing her hard across the seat. "On the floor! Stay down!"

But Cathy was thinking, *Alive!* He was supposed to be dead but he was alive! Somehow that impossibility seemed to relate to Jack, and there seemed to be hope, as astonishing and improbable as it was. But then there was another explosion, and the back windshield of the car starred into thousands of round-edged pieces.

Dave exclaimed, "Jesus Christ!" The starter screamed and Cathy doubled over, her hands covering her head.

The car lurched backward, slamming Cathy's head into the dashboard, then spun around, throwing her shoulder hard against the door. A third bullet screeched off the metal fender and Dave muttered, "Shit!" Then, "Hold on. I haven't driven like this since I was a teenager."

He pressed the gas and the tires squealed as the car swung across the parking lot.

It would have been a blatant untruth to say Cathy wasn't frightened. Adrenaline surged through her and her pulse roared, and incredulity mingled with shock to form a peculiar state of numbed horror; but the stark, raw-edged terror that had afflicted her for most of the night was gone. Perhaps she had reached a point beyond terror, perhaps she had simply learned to deal with it, or perhaps it was because she was no longer alone. Beneath the fear she was thinking clearly, beneath the adrenaline rush she was aware. She heard the tires scream and felt the back end of the car sway as Dave made a reckless left turn, and she heard the tone of the pavement beneath the tires change as the roadway did. Finally, when the car's speed grew steady and the fishtailing turns ceased, she eased up in her seat.

The road was dark before her, punctuated on either side with the faint gray outlines of trees that seemed to be passing much too fast, much too close. They were driving without lights. She gripped the upholstery, pressing her lips tightly together, and did not look at the driver. Instead she cast a quick glance over her shoulder, where she was sure she would see a car following them at the same breakneck speed.

She saw nothing.

"Kreiger," she managed at last. Her voice was tight and breathless. "It was him, it had to be—"

"It was him," Dave agreed grimly. His knuckles were white on the steering wheel, his expression fierce with concentration as he peered at the darkened slice of road ahead of them. "How did you leave him?"

The question was more of a command than a request, and Cathy answered as succinctly as she could. "I—he took me to a dirt road, beside a vineyard. I don't know where it was, I wasn't watching. . . . I had tear gas and I managed to get away, but he chased me. I hit him with a tool handle. I—I couldn't knock him out, but I got his gun."

As she spoke, a strange duality overtook her. Part of her stood aside, listening with incredulity and admiration to the tale of adventure. Another part of her relived it with all the drama and the terror her words could never convey, and that part understood the implications of what had just happened at the truck stop. She tried to keep her voice steady as she said, "How did he find me? How *could* he have found me?"

Cautiously, hoping the action would not be his

last, Dave reached forward and switched on the headlights. He kept his eye on the rearview mirror. Nothing happened. He flashed his brakes. No gleam of metal appeared in the reflected light. As far as he could see, they were alone on the winding stretch of country road. He relaxed a fraction, allowing himself to concentrate on details beyond the scope of their immediate survival.

He glanced quickly at Cathy and did not like what he saw lurking in the back of her eyes. So far she had inspired nothing but amazement in him; she had coped with and survived more than he ever would have given her credit for, and as much as he would have liked to tell her it was over, and everything was going to be all right, he couldn't. The worst had only begun and he couldn't afford for her to fold now.

He said, "He must have followed you."

She shook her head, her voice low and dull. "He couldn't have, I would have seen him. But it doesn't matter what I do, does it? He just keeps coming and coming . . ."

Dave said sharply, "He's not the goddamn Terminator. He followed you, that's all. How did you get to the truck stop?

"I walked—along the side of the freeway, until I saw the exit . . ."

"Then that's it. You wouldn't have been hard to spot. He got off at the first exit and waited for you."

"Then why didn't he kill me when I first got

there? Why wait until—"

"He doesn't want to kill you until you've told him what he wants to know." He darted a look at her. "You didn't tell him, did you?"

Cathy felt the fine muscles just beneath the surface of her skin begin to tense. Another car, another stranger, and the interrogation began again. She said stiffly, "No."

He nodded once. "Smartest thing you ever did in your life, trust me."

But she didn't. She couldn't. It could all be starting over again, and she couldn't run anymore. . . . She turned in her seat, looking at him steadily. "I guess you want to know, too."

Dave gave a dry little snort of amusement. "Believe me, lady, that's the last thing I want. People with that kind of information don't live very long."

And then, as though suddenly realizing how that sounded, he cast her an uncomfortable, apologetic look. But Cathy barely noticed. It was possible. He could be exactly who he claimed to be. Maybe he wanted nothing from her. Maybe he was just doing his job. Maybe he was on her side.

She said, "But . . . he tried to kill me back there."

Dave's face was tight and sober. "Not you. Me."

Already she was shaking her head. "But that still doesn't explain how he found me."

"He had to have followed you. It's the only

thing that makes sense." But he couldn't keep back a small frown as something else occurred to him, something distinctly unpleasant. "Either that, or . . ." He said that much before he realized it might be best to keep his speculation to himself. He glanced at her guiltily but she wasn't so easily put aside.

"What?" she demanded.

"Nothing."

"What, damn it! I'm the one he's after, don't you think I have a right to know?"

Dave was encouraged by her anger, though he would have preferred not to be the one to cause it. She was right: if either one of them was to survive, they couldn't start keeping secrets from one another.

"He could have monitored my cellular phone, when you called," he admitted reluctantly. "It's not that hard to do."

Cathy stared at him through the shifting patches of gray and dark. "He can do that?" Slowly, she felt the energy drain out of her, and with it, hope. If he had that kind of technology, that kind of power . . . then he was unstoppable. He might as well be the Terminator.

Dave kept his eyes firmly on the road. "Kreiger is a rogue government agent. I don't know how many contacts he has on the inside, or what kind of information or equipment he has access to. I think at this point we have to assume he can do just about whatever he wants to."

Cathy sank back against the seat, feeling limp and beaten. She knew there was more she should ask, more she needed to know, but the details, at that moment, seemed unimportant. She knew too much already, and everything she learned only made the nightmare loom larger.

After a time she said, a little hoarsely, "But we've lost him now. Nobody's following."

Again, Dave wanted to remain silent, to agree with her, to keep the worst to himself. But after all she had been through, she deserved more. "He doesn't have to follow. He'll put out an APB on the car and throw up roadblocks. We won't get out of the county."

Dave looked at her, but she was staring out the window. Her profile, what he could see of it, was unreadable. He wondered if she had even heard him.

After another moment he had his answer, but it was not what he expected, or wanted. "Take me to my car." Her voice was dull, and the words were spoken with the methodical deliberation commonly found in the drunk and the exhausted. "I have to get to the hospital. My brother was in an accident."

"I know. I'll get you there as soon as possible. But your car is even better known than mine. We have to—"

"My purse," she said. "I've got to get my purse back. My keys, my money, my driver's license . . . you can't even cash a check without a driver's license."

Dave felt the skin at the back of his neck prickle. *Don't do it, Cathy,* he thought. *Don't lose it on me now. We've got a long way to go and I can't carry you the rest of the way . . .*

He said carefully, "Cathy, listen to me."

She turned her face toward him. He glanced at her and was surprised by what he saw. Her face was pale, and shiny in places with tears, but her expression was calm, her eyes rational. She said softly, "I know. Somebody's trying to kill me and I'm worried about cashing a check. But sometimes it's easier to think about the small things."

She took a breath, and squared her shoulders. "So," she said, looking up at him in the dark, "what do we do now?"

Dave thought he had never admired anyone as much as he did Cathy Hamilton at that moment, and he wished he had a better answer. "The best we can," he said.

She swallowed hard and looked away. "What if it's not good enough?"

"It will be." His hands tightened on the wheel. "This time, it will be."

Dave pulled onto a rutted dirt trail that might once have been a logging road, or perhaps simply a farmer's access track, and switched off the lights. He monitored the police band as long as he dared, hoping to find out where the roadblocks were being established. But he should have known Kreiger wouldn't make a mistake like that. He, and the county police who were undoubtedly under his command, were maintaining radio silence.

He knew that every minute they stayed with the car only increased the danger they were in, but he hated to abandon it. The radio might not be much use now, but it — or the car phone — could mean life or death down the road. So would the dome light. They were safe here for now but come daylight the woods would be thick with uniforms, and a dragnet like that could keep them trapped indefinitely. Except Cathy Hamilton would not let herself be trapped, and she wouldn't stay here.

Dave glanced at her. Cathy Hamilton had an agenda that was more important than anything he could explain to her, more important even than her life, as she had proven more than once tonight. She was not going to stay still and hide while her brother lay dying. If Dave wanted to keep her with him and keep her safe, he was going to have to keep moving — and moving in the right direction.

He said, "We're going to have to walk from here."

Cathy jumped when he spoke, and instinctively her hand darted to the doorhandle, preparing for flight. She saw the surprise in his eyes when he noted the movement, and guilt rushed in to replace the panic that had surged so briefly. While he listened to the radio, she had been sitting there trying not to remember that other police radio, that other law official, that other dark road. This man had given her no reason to distrust him . . . but neither had Kreiger, until it was almost too late. And she could be foolish for believing what he said just because he had a kind voice. Yet . . . who else was there? Jack would have known what to do, but Jack was not there, and Cathy was so tired; she couldn't think straight any more . . .

That was when he spoke, startling her.

Ashamed, she shifted her eyes away and tried to slide her hand unobtrusively to the arm rest. She cleared her throat. "Where?"

He opened his own door. "We're going to have to switch vehicles. There was a used car lot just off the freeway. If we cut across country here we should come up behind it in about half a mile."

Cathy hesitated. "In the dark?"

He surprised her then with a grin. "Don't worry. I was a boy scout."

It seemed like a lifetime since Cathy had last seen anyone smile, since there had last been anything in the world to smile about. And before she knew it she felt her own lips softening in a weak response. It felt good.

Dave took from the car a couple of flashlights and some maps. He zipped the maps into the front pocket of his windbreaker, and handed one of the flashlights to Cathy. He unlocked the trunk and hesitated a moment, looking down, then he took out a shotgun. He glanced at

Cathy, but she said nothing and neither did he. They set off through the woods, Dave leading the way.

Even if Cathy had wanted to talk, she could not have found the breath, and merely staying on her feet required all the concentration at her command. Until that moment she had not realized how close to the mountains they were; the terrain was rocky and sometimes so steep that it was easier to slide down an incline than walk. At Dave's warning she kept her flashlight hooded and pointed directly at the ground beneath her feet, but even then she was certain the lights would be spotted, bobbing along the hillside, particularly as they moved close enough to hear the freeway again.

When Dave signaled her to turn off her flashlight she did so, and was surprised to find that her eyes had adjusted to the night enough to allow her to see without it. After a moment she realized it wasn't just her eyes; the night was fading, and it was almost dawn.

"We're cutting it close," Dave muttered.

He led the way out of the shadow of the woods and down a sloping bank to a dirt cutaway. Less than five hundred yards away was the chain-link fence that marked the back of the car lot.

Cathy was breathing hard as they reached it. She watched Dave grab the mesh and give it a shake, as though testing its strength, and that was the first time she realized what he intended to do.

"You're—not going to break in?"

"No need."

He moved quickly along the perimeter of the fence and Cathy had to run a little to keep up. Even then she didn't want to believe it, she tried not to think it, she tried not to let it matter.

The fence ended at the sides of a narrow prefab office building. Even Cathy could see that all a burglar had to do was break into the office, walk out the back door, and drive away with anything on the lot. Dave moved toward the building but Cathy stopped where she was.

She said flatly, "You're going to steal a car."

He went up the two narrow steps and rattled the knob, testing the lock and the weight of the door. "You have a better idea?"

Cathy stood still, hugging her arms and trying to keep her voice steady. "You said you were a cop. A policeman wouldn't—"

"This policeman's going to do what he has to to get out of here."

"You can't steal a car!" Her voice was growing shrill. "They'll know who did it, they'll follow us! We're in enough trouble already, you can't—"

"I'll leave a goddamn credit card, all right?"

He snapped his head around to her, and the minute he spoke he regretted his harsh words. She stood in the yard a few feet away from him, her face white and her eyes huge, unconsciously holding herself together by the force of her arms wrapped around her waist—a lone woman whose world had been jerked out from under her and who was trying to make it right again in the only way she knew how. Policemen don't steal cars. A simple rule that, when all others were shattered, she should have been able to count on. He wished he could tell her that he understood. He wished he could make it right for her. But every minute they delayed decreased their chances of getting out of here logarithmically, and he simply didn't have time.

So he said instead, "Get ready to run. There might be an alarm."

He wrapped his hand in the hem of his windbreaker and tapped the glass panel in the door with his fist. The shattering, tinkling sound it made as it hit the floor inside sounded loud enough to wake the dead, but no alarm went off.

Cathy watched as he reached inside and unlocked the door. She wanted to run. She wanted to run as far away from this place, and him, as she could possibly get. She wanted to stop having to choose who to trust and who to fear, who wore the white hat and who wore the black, at every turn. She knew she was being stupid about the car; after the things she had done tonight she should be the first to admit the old rules didn't apply. She wanted to believe in *him;* she needed to believe in him. Why couldn't he make it easy for her?

And then it was almost as though he read her mind. He turned back to her, and he held out the shotgun. His voice was gruff with the effort to sound casual. "Here," he said. "Hold this for me, will you?"

She couldn't see his face in the dark, but she knew the significance of the gesture, and read it in his voice. Trust.

After a moment Cathy stepped forward and took the heavy weapon from him. She, too, tried to keep her voice casual, as though nothing of significance had happened at all. "Why didn't you just jimmy the lock?"

"I was absent the day they taught that in rookie school."

Dave opened the door, using his flashlight in a brief crisscross pattern to find the landmarks he needed, then switching it off. Bob's Used Cars wasn't much different from Caleb's Super Deals back home: a big desk on the right wall, a couple of comfortable chairs for the customers, some file cabinets, a short hallway leading to the restrooms, and just inside that hallway a pegboard where the keys were hung. The difference was that Caleb had locked those keys inside a private office in back, but that still hadn't kept a couple of kids each year from going joyriding at his expense.

He moved as quickly as possible toward the shadow that was the hallway. Once there, he felt it safe to turn on his flash long enough to examine the rows of keys. The first one he took was for the padlock on the gate. Almost at random he snatched up the keys for an '87 Nova. He was just about to pocket them both when a sound, horribly unmistakable, deadly in intent, froze him where he stood.

It was a low, wet growl, only a few feet away, followed almost immediately by the rushing click of claws on linoleum. Dave thought, *Shit!* and spun away, but too late. The Doberman launched itself at his throat.

After standing alone and exposed in the yard for approximately twenty seconds, Cathy moved up onto the porch and then, hesitating, she stepped over the threshold. She could see the brief glint of Dave's flashlight in the hallway, backlighting his face as he examined the keys. Her teeth were tightly clenched with the effort to keep from urging him to hurry. She darted her eyes from the backdoor exit opposite the desk, through which they would have to leave, to the door she had come through, from which anyone could sneak up behind her. She thought about silent alarms and routine patrols and night-watchmen with sawed-off shotguns. She never once thought about guard dogs.

When it happened it was over in an instant, though it seemed to spin out forever. Dave turned off the light as he started back toward her, and Cathy breathed a little easier. She edged toward the back door. Then the dog seemed to come out of nowhere, a blur of fur and gleaming teeth and the blood-curdling sounds of a carnivore at a feast. When Dave burst into the small front office where she stood she wasn't sure whether he was running or had been thrown; she couldn't tell whether the animal had fastened itself to him or was inches away from doing so. Dave had hunched his shoulders and flung his arms over his head to protect his throat and face, and the dog was at his shoulder.

Cathy did not even have the breath for a scream. As instinctively as she would slap at a stinging insect or kick at a thorny vine, she lunged forward with the stock of the shotgun and shoved hard at the dog. The movement was not enough to do any real harm but it distracted the dog for the split second it took for Dave to wrench away before the animal's powerful jaws could get a firm grip on his flesh. Dave shouted "Run!" and propelled her toward the back door.

She reached it before he did and the dog was on him again. She could hear growls that were worse than furious barking, growls that should have been accompanied by the rending of flesh and the spurting of blood; she could hear Dave's grunts and gasps for breath as he tried to fight off the dog and she could hear her own cries, for she was screaming now, sobbing as she fumbled with the door knob with one hand, gripping the shotgun in the other. Dave stumbled and fell against her, hard. She lost her grip on the door knob and heard Dave cry out in pain, but she dared not look at him. She grabbed the door knob but it wouldn't turn. She pulled it, pushed it, she couldn't find the lock . . .

Her hand fumbled over the deadbolt, recognized it, twisted it left, then right, then left again. The door flew open and she stumbled through. Dave flung himself after her, twisting around, trying to dislodge the dog long enough to reach the pistol in his holster, or the one zipped in his windbreaker. The dog broke for an instant, only to charge again, and this time the teeth were aimed for Dave's eyes.

If Cathy had started to run she could have reached the fence and been over it before the dog started after her; there was never any doubt of that. She was, in fact, already running, but she wasn't aware of making a conscious decision when she veered away from the fence, back toward Dave. She grabbed the barrel of the shotgun and swung it, with all the force of her forward momentum, toward the dog. The impact knocked the weapon from her hands. There was a horrid, high-pitched, staccato animal scream, and the *thunk* of the stock against the dog's ribs. That, of all the things she had had to do that night, was the hardest. The dog fell still, whimpering.

Dave pushed her from behind, and they ran for the gate. Dave's breath was as harsh as hers as he fumbled to get the key in the padlock. When he dropped the key Cathy wanted to scream at him, until she saw that the reason he had lost his grip was because his hand was slick with blood. She sank to her knees beside him, sweeping the gravel-strewn ground with fingers that were shaking and numb. But she found the key first, grabbed it, and got it into the lock. Dave pushed and the gate swung open.

Pulling her by the arm, he moved swiftly down the rows of cars. Cathy's heart was pounding so hard now she couldn't even hear the gasping sobs of her breath. They both knew that the open lot would be a far more likely spot for an attack dog than the inner office had been.

Finally Dave, glancing back and forth between the numbers on the key tag and the numbers on the dealer's plates, said, "Here." He stopped before a white Nova and jerked open the driver's door.

Cathy started around to the passenger side, but suddenly her legs wouldn't carry her anymore. Suddenly she heard again in her mind that high, cut-off squeal, felt the ache in her biceps where the force of the blow had traveled through her arms and sent the weapon spinning, and she was seized with a chill that left her shaking. She staggered a few feet away, fell to her hands and knees in the gravel, and was violently sick.

For a long time after the spasm had passed she stayed there, weeping softly while the night spun around her. She felt weak, helpless. Then she felt a gentle hand on her shoulder, and Dave passed her a handkerchief. For a moment she just looked at it, oddly struck by what a sweet, old-fashioned gesture that was. So few men carried handkerchiefs any more. Then she took it, blotting her face.

She looked at Dave, too mentally worn out to

be embarrassed, too physically spent to feel much of anything at all. But she was struck — she couldn't help being struck just then, in the low gray light of predawn — by how kind his face looked. As kind as his voice.

She dropped her eyes. "I lost your gun."

"Yeah. Well . . ." With a gentle pressure on her arm, he helped her to her feet. "I hope you'll understand if I don't go back for it."

Cathy almost smiled.

Then his face, and his tone, became very serious. "Cathy," he said. "I've got to ask you to do something. I wish I didn't have to, but I don't see any other way."

She tensed. *No,* she thought. *No more. Don't ask me to be brave anymore, to think anymore, to do anything more, not tonight. I can't, not tonight . . .*

He said, "There's no way we're going to get out of here without going through at least one roadblock. They might not have very good physical descriptions, but they'll be doing license checks. I have an undercover ID, so I have to drive. They'll be looking for a man and a woman together, so the safest way to do this is for you to get in the trunk."

She waited. He said nothing more.

"That's it?"

He nodded. "It won't be long. An hour at most."

Again, Cathy almost managed a smile. "I thought it was going to be something hard."

"If they search the trunk it will be. But traffic's starting to pick up, and I'm counting on their not taking time to do that." He scanned the lightening sky briefly. "There's still a chance we can slide out of this. Maybe even bypass the roadblock."

Cathy shook her head tiredly. "You're driving, that's all I have to know."

She walked around to the trunk of the car, but then the false sense of ease she had felt began to evaporate. It was small, and airless, and to be locked in the dark for an indeterminate time . . . maybe forever . . . it was a frail plan, a stupid plan. There had to be a better way.

But when she glanced back at Dave she saw the tension around his eyes and the dark worry within them, and she knew they did not have the luxury, or the time, to come up with a better plan. She forced a tight smile, gesturing toward the trunk. "Have you got a key for this thing?"

Chapter Twelve

Cathy tried not to think about coffins. She tried not to think about how badly she wanted to stretch out her legs, or what would happen if she got a cramp, or how quickly the trunk could fill up with carbon monoxide, or what would happen if Dave were stopped, or killed, and no one ever let her out of there. She tried not to count the minutes. She tried to pretend she was anywhere other than where she was. And it took forever.

Actually, it took less than ten minutes. Though he hadn't had time to do much more than glance at the map, Dave figured a town the size of Hinesville wouldn't have more than two or three freeway exits at the most, and all of them would be covered. Two cars were waiting to pass the roadblock when he got on the entrance ramp, and he knew he'd been right. The suspense was almost over.

He had taken off his windbreaker and his hat—two identifying garments Kreiger might remember—and hidden them in the trunk with Cathy. His shoulder harness and pistol he slipped into the glove compartment. He didn't know whether he'd use the gun if he had the chance. It was too soon to worry about the car's having been reported stolen; they would have at least a three-hour head start before anyone even noticed it was missing.

It was over in a matter of minutes. He had his license ready—the one that identified him as Jeff Hopper of Portersville, California—and had no trouble putting on the half-annoyed, half-anxious look of the ordinary motorist who was stopped at this hour of the morning. He had, after all, seen that look enough times himself.

He didn't think about Cathy at all, cramped up in the trunk with the smell of exhaust, and the sound of the road in her ears, without even enough room to turn over or shift her arms. It was almost as though thinking about her would have somehow magically revealed her presence to their enemies, and besides, the only way to play an undercover was to believe it. So he rolled down the window, leaning his elbow on the frame with his license in his hand as he inched toward the waiting officer, and when he reached him he said, "What's going on?"

The officer took his license, examined it with a flashlight, and glanced at Dave and back at the license. "Escaped fugitive," he said. "There's been a shooting."

"Jeez. What's this world coming to, huh?"

181

"Yes, sir."

The officer shined the flash in the back seat and around the floor. Another car pulled onto the ramp, its lights flashing in Dave's mirror, and slowed abruptly when the flashing blue dome light came into view. The officer returned the license.

"Have a good day, sir. Drive carefully."

"Hope you guys catch him."

Dave pulled forward, building up speed for the freeway. Sometimes things went right. Sometimes the bad guys *didn't* win. Sometimes ordinary people made ordinary judgments, like not asking for the car registration with the license, like not walking around the car to notice a trunk that wasn't quite closed, like not knowing or remembering that Portersville, California was also where the fugitive was from. Sometimes you got a break. Sometimes you slid by.

The road sang beneath the wheels. He watched his speed. They weren't out of the woods yet, and if he got stopped for speeding there would be a registration check. But he wanted to speed. He wanted to push the little car 'til its wheels shuddered, to beat that daylight that was coming up on them too fast. He wanted to stop and let Cathy out, and that was the need he fought the hardest. If he got off the freeway again he might not be so lucky next time; if he pulled over he'd only draw attention to himself. Anyone might see, anything might happen, and they dared not take a chance.

Cathy understood that. She knew she had to stay put until they made the final exit off the freeway. It would be less than an hour, if his guesses were right. Dave hated small places, and he knew every minute must seem like an eternity to her. He tried not to think about that. And he tried not to think about how Cathy would react when she found out where he was taking her, which was nowhere near where she wanted to be.

The changing of the texture of the road aroused Cathy from a stupor that was induced by exhaustion and monotony, fear and discomfort. First there had been the freeway, then an exit, and she thought Dave would stop and open the trunk. But the car picked up speed again, on a paved road with many twists and turns. She didn't know why but she got the feeling they were climbing. Maybe she could detect the subtle strain of the engine or the downshifting of gears, or maybe she was imagining it. Then there came the gravel road, and that was what jarred her out of the half-dozing, half-hypnotic state into which she had retreated. The road was badly rutted, and every time the wheels bounced her shoulder hit the tire well, or her head rapped painfully against the trunk lid, or her hip banged the floorboard, and it went on for a very long time. But it wasn't the discomfort that alarmed Cathy. They should not have been on a gravel road. There *were* no gravel roads between Hinesville, California and Albany, Oregon, that much she knew. Why had they left the highway? Where *were* they?

She didn't know what she was speculating or what the worst might be, but it comforted her to be able to reach Dave's windbreaker, to feel the pistol he had zipped in the pocket, to wrap her hand around it. When she thought about how many of the night's horrors had been directed by weapons, and how badly every encounter with them had ended for her, she did not know why there should be any reassurance at all in the presence of the gun. But there was, nonetheless.

The car stopped. She moved her hand, as much as possible, to bring the nylon-wrapped pistol closer. She felt the shifting of weight as Dave left the car, the click of his door closing. His footsteps made no sound, so she knew the car had left the gravel. She could smell pine and spruce. She tried not to think the worst. She tried to be prepared for it.

Dave cut the shoestring with which he had tied the trunk, leaving room for air circulation, and the lid swung open creakily. Cathy wanted to spring to the ground, ready to run, but she could hardly straighten her legs. It took a moment for her eyes to adjust to the gray light that filtered over her.

Dave reached in to help her as she struggled to sit up. "You okay?"

She lost her hold on the windbreaker, and the gun slipped back onto the floorboard. She nodded, tripping despite Dave's support as she climbed over the back bumper. It was morning—

184

the barest edge of morning but morning nonetheless. The air was damp, foggy and a little chill. Despite the heavy cloak of evergreens that surrounded them, it was light enough to see clearly. What Cathy saw was that they were at the end of some kind of rutted trail in the middle of the woods. The fog was coming from a lake that lapped against the side of the bank about two hundred yards below them. Before them was some kind of structure—a small shed or shack with peeling cedar shingles, dirty windows and a rusty tin roof.

Before she could speak, Dave said, "This is a fishing cabin I own. We're safe here. It was dangerous to stay on the road much longer, you know that, don't you? We had to find a place to—"

"Hide out," she finished tonelessly. But as quiet as her voice was, it seemed to echo in the stillness. It was so isolated here, so empty. Anything could happen and no one would ever know. No one.

"I know I promised to take you to your brother. I will. But we're going to have to wait here until I figure out the safest way to do that."

He was still holding her arm. Wordlessly, she pulled away.

He stepped in front of her. He was almost half a foot taller than she and he had to bend his neck to look at her. His face was lined with exhaustion and his voice was intent. "Cathy," he said, "you believe me, don't you?"

She looked at him steadily for a long time. Then she said, "Of course."

The minute she said it she knew it was true. She started walking toward the shack.

The night was over. Cathy felt the daylight on her eyelids, and that was the first thing she thought: *It's over. Thank God, it's over.* At first she didn't remember why.

She opened her eyes, and then she remembered. The cot on which she lay was narrow and lumpy; it smelled musty even though she had seen Dave take the clean sheets from a cupboard and she had put them on herself. The window opposite was cloudy with grease and half-obscured by a sagging shade, but it allowed enough light to penetrate that Cathy could tell it was late morning, perhaps even afternoon. With a jolt that hurt her chest she came fully awake, and as the memories of the night returned waves of panic spread through her stomach and out to her limbs like ripples in a pond. It wasn't over. She wasn't safe. Hours were gone, wasted; people were still trying to kill her, she was stranded without a car or money in this strange place, and Jack . . . what had happened to Jack? She had to get to him, he was depending on her, and she was no closer to reaching him than she ever had been. Her purse was gone, her car was gone, she was alone in the middle of nowhere . . .

The last thought sent a shaft of ice-cold terror through her veins, because for a moment she thought it might be true. She sat up abruptly, and before her feet hit the floor she saw him.

He was standing at a counter at the opposite end of the room, spooning instant coffee into a cup of hot water. "I know," he said without turning, "the place is a mess. Somehow it doesn't seem so bad when it's just a bunch of men sitting around in smelly fishing clothes."

He brought the coffee to her, leaving the spoon in the cup. "No cream, but there's some sugar somewhere if you want it."

Cathy shook her head, pushing her hair back from her face with one hand and accepting the coffee with the other. It was a thick crockery mug, hand-glazed, perfectly suited for the rustic cabin, yet oddly out of place. It was the kind of thing a woman might shop the mountain fairs and country craft shows for, but a man would never think to buy.

Dave put a fresh pan of water to heat on the hot plate and returned to her with his own cup. There was another cot opposite hers, and he sat on the edge of it, facing her. Cathy wondered whether he had slept at all. From the looks of him, the answer was no.

She stirred the coffee absently, waiting for the steam to dissipate, looking at the man across from her. She thought, *He looks like a cop*—and what that meant, she wasn't entirely sure. He had a face that was neither handsome nor unhandsome, the kind of face that defied description because it was simply so ordinary. The kind of face that could blend in with a crowd, which Jack had once told her, from his vast store of spy novel information, was an essential characteristic in an undercover policeman or a secret agent. His eyes were brown, now deeply pocketed with weariness and bracketed with lines that probably were not, on other occasions, as prominent as they were today. His cheeks were stubbled with beard, his hair was thick and brown and rumpled. Though now he looked older, Cathy figured him to be in his late thirties.

He was looking at her in the same quiet, unaffected way as she was looking at him, resting his elbows on his knees, holding the coffee cup loosely between his hands. Both of them knew what had to be said, but neither of them wanted to begin. Cathy sipped from the mug and wondered who was the woman who had thought of him at a mountain crafts show.

After a moment he said, "There's nothing to eat — nothing you'd want to chance, anyway. But there's a little country store not too far from here, we can walk up there in awhile."

Cathy said, "I need to call —"

"I know. There's a pay phone."

They sat for a while longer, sipping coffee. It was slightly stale and had a dull bitter aftertaste, the way most instant coffees do, but it was hot and strong and gradually began to restore Cathy's strength. After a moment Dave got up to refill his cup, but when he gestured to Cathy questioningly she shook her head.

He took his time measuring out the coffee, stirring it. Then he crossed the room again and stood at the cloudy window opposite Cathy's bunk, looking out at the lake.

"We had a call," he said, "From a woman named Laura, about a drug deal that was supposed to go down last night. We never met her, we never saw her, we didn't even know her name until later. We just knew that she was going to take a call at that phone booth that would give her the specifics, then she was going to turn the information over to us."

Cathy saw his shoulders lift in a half-shrug. "A lot of unanswered questions in a situation like that. You believe about half of what you hear, you never know what to expect. I was surprised to see anybody show up at that phone booth at all."

It took Cathy a moment to absorb the implications, to make sense of what, at any other time, would have been a ridiculously simple scenario. "You thought I was Laura."

He nodded. "What're the odds, huh? That you would show up where you did, when you did . . ."

Cathy said nothing. She could hardly even think.

"Toby—my partner—he expected you to go willingly. He wasn't prepared for any gunplay. Neither was I. But it must've looked like you were being forced. Deke, the man I . . ." There was a pause, and he lifted the cup to his lips. It was longer than it should have been before he continued. "The other man—his job was to protect you, or the woman he thought was Laura. He had no choice but to open fire. He was an undercover agent. I didn't know that until later." There was a long silence, and still he didn't turn around. Then he said softly, "Jesus, what a screwup."

"Screwup," Cathy repeated flatly, staring into her coffee. "Yes, I would say that." Her hands tightened around the mug, slowly, tendons showing white and veins pulsing blue. She fought to keep her voice steady but it rose on every word. "I've been chased, shot at, arrested, kidnaped—my life has been torn apart, my car's impounded, my purse is stolen, my brother is in the hospital and I don't even know whether he's alive or dead, all because you *screwed up*, isn't that right? My God! You mistook me for a woman you'd never even seen! You started shooting at people you didn't even know! Screwup? Yeah, I'd say you screwed up, wouldn't you?"

She stopped, because she was afraid if she said any more she would become incoherent. She brought her fingers to her lips, pressing hard as though to literally hold back words, and was surprised to see her hand was trembling. She could see Dave's shoulders tightening, as though her accusations were physical blows, with every word she spoke, and though she knew she should be sorry she wasn't. Her anger was a magnificent thing, fierce and energizing and right, and she wouldn't apologize for it. For one brief perverse and satisfying moment she let herself revel in it.

Dave stood at the window, silent and unmoving, while the sting of her bitterness faded slowly from the air. Cathy took a sip of coffee. She made herself swallow it. She said after a long time, in a deliberately calm voice, "What about the real Laura? What happened to her?"

"Kreiger killed her."

She stared at him, outrage forgotten, resentment abandoned, even fear put aside in the simple shock of that matter-of-factly uttered statement.

He lifted his coffee cup, turning now to face her. Backlit by the sun, his face looked even more haggard, his eyes haunted by exhaustion and a bitterness of his own. Cathy felt something twist inside her, reaching out in sympathy to him. She was sorry, then.

"At least that's what I figure," he went on. "He knew she was dead, that much is certain. My theory is he followed her to the rendezvous at the convenience store, saw his chance, and wasted her right there, planning to step in and take the call himself. But you got in the way."

Cathy's head was spinning. "That man — the black man who got shot . . . he was trying to warn me. Or her. He said 'It's off for tonight, babe. You've been made.' "

Dave's attention quickened briefly, then he nodded. "He knew about Kreiger, then. But he was taking a hell of a chance, warning you. Because it wasn't really off, otherwise they wouldn't have made the call."

She frowned, running her fingers through her tangled hair. "But—the phone call. It didn't even make any sense. Just numbers and letters, nothing anybody could use."

"A code." He nodded thoughtfully. "Makes sense. Then he gave a shake of his head. "So you really *don't* know what the caller said. After all this, even if you wanted to tell what you know—you don't know anything."

Cathy lifted her eyes to him. There was a moment's hesitation, but no more. And afterward it never occurred to her to wonder whether she'd made the right decision. She said, "I said it didn't make sense, not that I didn't know what was said. I have a memory for details. I remember exactly what the caller said."

Dave held her gaze for a long and steady moment. She waited for him to ask. And he didn't.

Cathy went to the hot plate to refill her coffee cup, diluting the muddy mixture it already held. "So Kreiger really *is* a government agent. And he was just trying to cut in on this drug deal?" She spoke uncertainly, trying to give herself time to accept it. It all sounded too much like a television show to be real.

"Apparently he's been under suspicion for a

while. He was assigned to the Delcastle case under FBI surveillance, and he did exactly what they expected him to."

"Well at least somebody was expecting something." Then she turned. "Wait a minute. If the FBI knew—"

"Laura was the wild card. Nobody expected her to get pissed off at her boyfriend—Delcastle—and go to the local police. Not the FBI, not Kreiger, certainly not us. And when everybody arrived at the same spot at the same time . . ." He shrugged. "You can't tell the players without a scorecard."

Cathy leaned against the counter, cradling the coffee cup, not even trying to make sense of it all anymore. "So where's the FBI now? Why aren't they here when we need them? Why did they let Kreiger get away, why did they let him take me—surely *they* knew I wasn't Laura?"

The look Dave slanted in her direction seemed almost wry. "That fellow you left back in the parking lot of Two Mile Church? He was the agent in charge of the case. He won't be much help to anybody for a while."

Cathy felt her knees start to buckle, and if she had not been leaning against the counter she might well have fallen. That she *couldn't* accept. She thought of the terror of the road duel, the drawn gun, the *thunk* of the body hitting her car. . . . And he had been trying to help her. All the time, he had been her ally . . .

She felt the grip of Dave's fingers on her upper arm and saw the concern on his face, and she realized she must have grayed out for a minute after all. In an instant he had crossed the room and now was removing the coffee mug from her fingers, guiding her to a chair. "Here," he said. "Take it easy. Sit down."

She sank into the hard, ladder-backed chair, shaking. She brought her hand to her mouth, breathing deeply through her fingers. When she could speak she managed, "I could have—killed him."

Dave knelt beside her, pressing her coffee cup into her hand. "Here. Drink some."

She obeyed, and he watched her carefully. After a sip or two of the hot coffee she could feel the color return to her cheeks, and he must have noticed it as well. The concern on his face was replaced with satisfaction. He got to his feet. "I wouldn't worry too much about the FBI, if I were you. It was their idea to use you as bait."

She said hoarsely, "What?"

"That's why they let Kreiger get to you. They can't bust him until he steps out of line, and he can't make his move until he gets the information you have."

Cathy's throat was dry. Drug lords, rogue government agents, the FBI . . . She had done nothing to deserve any of this, nothing to invite it, but people she had never heard of were trying to kill her. All of them wanted something from her and none of them cared what they had to do to get it. And *none of it was her fault!*

She looked at Dave and said, her voice totally devoid of expression, "What about you? What do you want from me?" As soon as she spoke she wished she could take the words back — but was actually glad she couldn't. She needed to know. She had to ask.

Dave Jenks, she saw in that moment, was a man who had grown accustomed to hiding his feelings; he had done it so often that he was almost good at it. She saw the barest flicker of surprise in his eyes, but nothing more. He didn't answer right away, but neither did he avoid her eyes, or change his expression.

Finally he said, "I'm not sure. I guess the main thing I want from you is something you can't give me."

"What's that?"

He finished off his coffee and walked to the sink. "I don't know. Maybe . . . just a chance to even up the score."

Cathy knew there was a story behind that statement and she knew it was important. She wanted to ask what he meant, but didn't feel she had the right. As battered and misused as she was, she was still ashamed for mistrusting Dave.

She said instead, "What do we do now?"

Dave washed the cup and turned it upside down on the counter to drain. Cathy suspected that his delay in answering was because he wasn't sure what the answer was.

195

Then he turned, drying his hands on a paper towel, and almost managed a smile. "Right now," he said, "let's go get something to eat."

Chapter Thirteen

The truth was that Dave didn't know what they were going to do now. He had bought them a few hours safety here in the mountains, maybe more, but Cathy wouldn't stay here forever and he didn't blame her.

If life were fair and right, morning would have brought the intervention of the replacement FBI team, and with it a new strategy. Kreiger would have been apprehended; Dave and Cathy would be safe. But if life were fair Cathy Hamilton never would have ended up in this mess in the first place, and Dave wouldn't have had to risk his badge to get her out of it. So he wasn't counting on anything, and he was preparing for the worst.

While Cathy was sleeping he had hidden the car as best he could in the woods in back of the cabin. By now the car would have been reported stolen, and to try to use it would be suicidal, but he hadn't been able to force himself to push it into the lake, as he probably should have done.

Desperate measures were not second nature to him, as they might have been to others in his profession — Kreiger for instance — and he liked to think there was always a chance things wouldn't get as bad as they looked. They might need the car. They might find out the manhunt was off, Kreiger was in custody; and it was not in Dave's character to overreact.

But neither had he stayed in law enforcement as long as he had by playing the fool. He knew things could get a lot worse before they got better, and he had to be prepared.

They were taking a chance by going to the store, but in Dave's opinion it was minimal. He generally brought his own supplies when he visited the cabin and hardly ever came in here, so the proprietor didn't know him. If he were questioned later he might remember a man and a woman fitting their descriptions, but they weren't the only tourists on the lake, or even in the store. The chances were slim that they would ever be traced this far, although if they were . . . well, it was a calculated risk.

The unprepossessing little store was lined with narrow aisles containing an eclectic assortment of merchandise: dusty cans of foodstuffs, hiking boots, lantern wicks, paperback books with yellow, moisture-swollen pages. In the refrigerator case plastic containers of bait were stacked between cartons of milk and cans of biscuits; everything smelled like old wood and dampness.

It was the busy season at the lake. Dave counted seven other people in the store besides himself and Cathy: a family of three, two middle-aged men talking loudly and loading up on beer, and a young couple who looked like they might have posed for the cover of an L.L. Bean catalog and who, judging by the private smiles and secret touches they shared, were either on their honeymoon or not married at all. Cathy moved through the aisles with nervous distraction, and she kept glancing back at the telephone she had seen on the front porch. Dave stayed close to her, trying to cover her anxious behavior by acting normal.

But even he couldn't make himself linger, examining the oddities and grimacing over the prices the way the other shoppers were doing. He filled a hand-held basket with single-serving cans of stew, and tuna and fruit, boxes of cookies, crackers, and toaster pastries. When he came upon a display of dehydrated campers' meals, he tossed in a handful. Even Cathy began to look questioningly at his choices and the quantity, but it wasn't until Dave reached the register counter that he admitted even to himself what his plan was. In front of the register was a display of tackle, cheap cotton hats, maps, and compasses. Behind the counter hung a selection of nylon backpacks and canteens. Dave added a compass and a selection of maps to his basket, and asked for a backpack and two canteens. When the total was rung up he was glad he had cashed his paycheck the day before. He asked for another two dollars in quarters for the telephone.

"What are you going to do with all that stuff?"

Cathy asked, *sotto voce,* as they left the store.

"Maybe nothing. I hope nothing." He poured the quarters into her hand and nodded to the telephone. "Make your call. Don't be long."

Cathy stared at the handful of change. "Don't you carry a phone card?"

He looked impatient. "I'd rather not leave a record if we can help it. And I'd also rather not stand around looking conspicuous. Hurry, will you?"

Cathy had to dial information for the number of the hospital, then wait for the operator to give her the charges. It took forever. Finally a voice answered, "Mercy Hospital."

The sound of that voice—proof positive that a world existed outside the endless jumble of impossible terrors that Cathy's world had become— seemed in that moment to be the sweetest thing Cathy had ever heard. She went weak with the sound of it, she closed her eyes and let it flow through her, and for a moment she couldn't even speak.

The voice repeated, "Hello, Mercy Hospital. May I help you?"

And there was another moment when Cathy didn't *want* to speak, when she was afraid of what she had to say and what the answer might be. But then she noticed Dave standing close to her and she felt the seconds ticking off while she struggled for her voice. Afraid of losing the connection, she blurted, "I—I'm calling about the condition of a patient. He was brought in last night. Jack Hamilton."

"One moment please."

Her hand tightened on the telephone. She waited. And she thought—she couldn't help thinking—about how it had all begun, with her hand gripping another receiver in another telephone booth, waiting. And how time seemed to have slowed down and started to slip backward, and maybe it really would never end . . .

Then the voice was back.

"Mr. Hamilton is listed in satisfactory condition in the critical care unit."

The relief that went through her literally tingled in her fingertips and caused dots of light to dance before her eyes. Until that moment she had believed, she had been sure . . . but Dave was right. He hadn't lied to her. Jack was alive. *He was alive!*

She knew then that the person on the other end was about to disconnect and she stammered hoarsely, "Wait—no. I need to—transfer me to someone on that floor. Please."

"One moment please."

She waited.

"ICU."

"This is Cathy Hamilton," she said quickly, acutely aware of how rapidly her three minutes were passing. "Jack Hamilton's sister. He was in an accident last night, and . . ."

"Yes." There seemed to be a note of accusation in the young woman's voice. "We've been trying to reach the family."

"There've been some problems. The children—"

"Just a minute, Miss Hamilton, I'm going to

have to transfer you to social services. We really don't have any information—"

"But my brother—can you tell me how he's doing, what—"

"He passed the night without incident. That's really all I can tell you over the phone. If you'd like to talk to Dr. Jamison—"

"Yes! Please."

"I'll have to take your number and let him return your call."

"But—"

There was a click and the operator interrupted, "Please deposit thirty cents for the next minute."

"I don't have a number," Cathy said frantically. "I'll have to call you back. When can I—"

There was another click, and then a dial tone.

Pressing her lips together furiously, Cathy dialed another series of numbers.

"This is collect from Cathy," she told the operator.

She waited, and waited. The phone began to ring. Twice, three times. *Be there, Ellen . . .*

There was a click and her own voice answered, absurdly cheerful. "Hello! We're so sorry to have missed your call—"

Damn it, Ellen, you promised!

The operator said, "I'm sorry, there doesn't seem to be—"

"That's my home number, I'll authorize the charges. Let me leave a message."

"I'll have to—"

The beep on the answering machine sounded and Cathy said over the operator, "Ellen, it's me.

I'm okay. I'm at—"

Dave's hand came down on the disconnect button.

With an inarticulate cry of outrage, Cathy twisted away from him, lifting the receiver as though to strike his hand away, and then she met his eyes and understood. She understood, and it made her feel weak, and ill. They had fled through the night to this safe haven and she had been about to give away their location. To leave a message on an answering machine tape that anyone could play . . .

She let Dave take the telephone receiver from her and replace it in its cradle. She said uncertainly, "Ellen should have been there. She promised she would stay there."

"Doesn't she have to work?"

"No. She's a teacher, like me. School recessed, last week. She wouldn't have gone home, knowing I was in trouble . . . she would have waited by the phone, she's that kind of person."

"Maybe she was in the shower."

"Maybe." She clasped her elbows against a sudden chill, and though she didn't want to say it, she had to. "You don't think—he has my house keys, he could have gone back there . . ."

Dave said, "I don't think he'd want to lose the time."

But there was a lack of conviction in his tone, an uneasiness in his eyes.

Cathy made herself go on, hugging her elbows tighter. "He knew there was someone at my house, didn't he? You knew it, you talked to Ellen, so he must have known. He could have gone back there, thinking she might know where I was, and when she didn't . . ."

Dave said shortly, "I've told you before, he's not Superman. Stop borrowing trouble."

But Cathy could tell by the troubled expression on his face that he did not think the scenario was as farfetched as he pretended, and she said tightly, "We can't go on not knowing. How can you stand not knowing? He could be anywhere, or nowhere. We've got to find out what's happening. We can't stay here forever!"

Though every cautious instinct he possessed rebelled against what he had to do, Dave knew Cathy was right, and he had known it since sunrise this morning. They couldn't go on stumbling around in the dark. While they hid out, waiting for something to happen and hoping they were safe, their margin of safety might be diminishing by the minute. He tried to rationalize that there was no security risk in letting Cathy phone the hospital; it was a perfectly natural thing for her to do, and she had said nothing that could lead anyone to her location. But if Dave made a phone call as well . . .

He had no choice. He had to know what was going on. Their survival might well depend on the accuracy of that information.

He handed Cathy the sack he carried and dug in his pocket for more change.

He dialed the chief's direct line. There was a chance that, after an all-night crisis, he might have gone home for some rest, and if that was the case Dave didn't want to risk anyone else answering the phone. But he knew his chief well enough to expect him to still be in the office, sleeping there, if necessary, for two or three days in a row. And he was right.

When he heard Hayforth's voice, he turned his back on Cathy in an automatic shielding gesture that was habitual for him while talking on the phone, and he murmured, "Hey, man. What's going on?"

There was a brief, startled silence. If he hadn't known better, Dave might have thought the chief didn't recognize his voice. But then the voice returned, dry and tense. "Maybe you could tell me."

Dave drew a soft breath. He had been afraid of that. "I guess you heard about my troubles."

"And I'll guess you've got more trouble than you know. A civilian was killed at that diner. You've got uniforms in two states looking for you, and you're a fool for calling here."

It seemed a long time before Dave could release his breath, and when he did it was in a whispered, "Shit!"

He pushed his hand across his jaw; he tried to think. He couldn't look at Cathy. "Look," he said, "I need some information."

"The only information I've got for you is this," the chief replied, his voice low. "We're talking about a thirty-million dollar deal, two high-powered government agencies, a three-year investigation, and repercussions that you and I aren't even smart enough to imagine. These people don't do business like we do, and certain players in this game are expendable. I wish it were different." There was a click, and silence.

Dave looked at the dead receiver. He said again, softly, "Shit," and he hung up the phone.

He took the sack from Cathy. "Let's go."

Cathy knew there was no point in asking him what he had learned, or even who he had called; from the look on his face she knew it wasn't good news, and he would tell her what he wanted to when he wanted to. She had her own priorities now, and they did not include waiting for Dave Jenks to take her into his confidence.

When she had walked into the fishing shack with him that dawn it had been with every intention of leaving him as soon as possible—not because she thought he meant her any harm, but because she was almost sure his intentions were the opposite. He wanted to protect her, and the best way to do that would be to keep her here, safe and hidden away. But Cathy couldn't stay here.

She had watched which pocket he put the car keys in, and had planned to slip them away from him as soon he was asleep. But exhaustion had claimed her first. That meant the plan had been delayed, but the urgency had only increased. Dave Jenks was not going to take her to Jack, and so she had to get away from him.

The crunching of their footsteps on the dirt path that wound away from the store was the only break in the silence until Dave spoke.

His voice, echoing the course of her thoughts, startled her. "How's Jack?"

She shot a quick glance at him. His expression was taut and his eyes were preoccupied, but the interest and concern that backed the question were genuine. Cathy felt a stab of irrational guilt, as though she had been caught plotting a betrayal—which, she supposed, in a way she was doing.

"When you say that," she answered slowly, still watching him, "it's like you know him. I felt the same way the first time I talked to you on the phone. Like you knew me."

Dave lifted his shoulders a little in a gesture that was almost embarrassed. "I guess I feel like I do know him—and you. I spent so much time studying you and trying to understand you last night—I had to, trying to stay one step ahead of you. And Jack is just a part of you."

Just a part of you. Never had she heard the relationship between twins expressed so simply, so elegantly, so precisely . . . and yet with a subtle nuance that no one else might have noticed, though to Cathy it made all the difference in the world. All her life she had been referred to, and had thought of herself, in relationship to Jack; Jack's sister, Jack's twin, aunt to Jack's children. Jack's confidante, Jack's cheerleader, Jack's Number One Fan . . . a part of Jack. No one had ever referred to Jack as just a part of Cathy before. No one.

She said, "He's still critical. They wouldn't tell me anything else and I couldn't talk to the doctor. I . . ." Her throat started to tighten, she had to squeeze the words out. "I thought he was dead. Since last night, I've thought . . . and it's still hard to believe, you know? That he's really alive."

A small frown of perplexity replaced the deeper anxiety that had haunted Dave's eyes since he hung up the phone. "Why did you think that? Did someone tell you that?"

She shook her head. The day that had begun so gray was clearing with afternoon, and patches of sunlight began to appear like yellow leaves in the tops of the trees, and in lacy patterns on the path. Even when they turned onto the trail that led through the woods and back to the cabin, Cathy could still see occasional scraps of sunlight breaking through the trees, outlining the bushes and turning the pinestraw to gold.

She said, "It's hard to explain about twins. Sometimes we can just — sense things about the other. And last night, while all that was happening, I just kept trying to think what Jack would do — God knows, I don't know anything about defensive driving or street fighting or thinking like a criminal, or even hiding from one — but Jack is always reading these action adventure books and spy novels. He's a virtual font of trivia about things like that. So I kept trying to think like he would, and sometimes it seemed I could actually hear him in my head, telling me what to do . . . just like he's always been there, all my life, helping me out, showing me how, telling me what to do when I didn't know which way to turn. I—I know this is going to sound crazy, but I honestly don't think I could have survived if it hadn't been for him, for the sound of his voice in my head, for the things I remembered him saying over the years. And then . . . after Kreiger, when I was so terrified, alone and lost in the dark, when I needed him most . . . Jack wasn't there anymore. That feeling was gone, the sound of his voice . . . I knew he was dead."

Dave stopped walking, and turned to look at her. Dappled light filtered through the feathery branches of a spruce and patterned his face, erasing the lines for a moment, softening the harshness. He said, "Cathy, don't you see what it is?"

She had spoken, putting her innermost thoughts into words, without ever meaning to tell him so much, and hardly aware, at the time, of doing it. Now she felt uncomfortable, uncertain, and she shifted her eyes away.

His tone was gentle, but insistent with quiet confidence as he went on. "It was never Jack at all. *You're* the one who eluded a highly trained FBI agent, not once, but twice. *You're* the one who called for help and then had sense enough to realize—which God knows is more than I did at the time—that the very people you called might be at the root of your troubles. You're the one who was strong enough, and smart enough, to disable an armed man, and you're the one who had the compassion to call for an ambulance even though it endangered your escape. Maybe it was easier for you to pretend it was Jack, but when you fought off Kreiger and got away—

209

something I would have given you one chance in a thousand of doing—even your subconscious must have finally realized you could take care of yourself. You didn't *need* Jack anymore."

She didn't like that, even though she recognized a solid element of truth beneath what he said, even though she was astonished by the sensitivity that allowed him to say it and the depth of understanding he seemed to possess of a woman he had met less than six hours ago. But not need Jack? . . . That was ridiculous. That, he didn't understand.

She started walking again, drawing a deep breath. "I've got to get to him. I—it was a head injury, you know. He could be paralyzed or—or have permanent brain damage, or be in a coma for weeks or months, or . . ." *Not come out of it at all* were the words she couldn't say. *Be a vegetable for the rest of his life* was what she couldn't think. Or he could die tomorrow, tonight, within the hour, without ever having seen her, without giving her a chance to say goodbye.

Except he wasn't going to die. She knew that now. And if she could only reach him, she would be sure of it . . .

Dave said, "How old are the kids?"

She recognized the attempt at distraction and was grateful for it. He had no answer for any of the horrors she had suggested, no comfort to offer or reassurances to pour forth. But he was right; there was no point in torturing herself with uncertainties when she couldn't affect things one way or the other. She had to concentrate on reaching Jack, on helping him get well, on giving back to him what he had given to her, so generously, all his life.

"Five," she answered. "They're twins, you know. A girl and a boy. It happens that way in families sometimes, the twin gene or whatever it is." They passed at that moment through a shadow, and the chill seemed to go through her soul as she added quietly, "They must be terrified."

"Yes," Dave agreed simply, and she was grateful for that too. "But kids are pretty resilient. They'll be okay."

They came to a break in the trees, and until then Cathy hadn't realized how high up they were. Below them about five hundred yards was the cabin, and the lake glinting in all directions. Beyond her left shoulder were the blue-gray shoulders of mammoth mountains, and directly below, winding down in an almost endless spiral, was the road by which they had come. Cathy could see all the way to the blacktop highway, and beyond, to a cluster of rooftops that could have indicated a small town.

She said, "Where are we?"

"A place called Crystal Point Lake. Oregon."

Hope leapt as she turned to him. "Then we aren't far—"

He shifted the sack of merchandise to his other arm, and moved his gaze away. "About a hundred miles."

She stared at him. She didn't know why she was surprised. She was naïve to expect anything else. "That's too far. I was closer to my brother last night."

Dave turned his eyes back to her again, quiet, regretful, but certain. He said, "You know Kreiger will be waiting for you at the hospital, don't you?"

She swallowed hard. "No. I don't know that."

"He knows where you're headed. If he can't cut you off before then, you can be sure he'll meet you there. Do you really want to take a chance on leading him straight to Jack? To the children?"

God. Her throat was dry, convulsing with such suddenness she couldn't even speak the word. Even now he might have reached them, he might . . .

Dave saw the panic rising in her eyes and he said firmly, "He's going to wait for you to surface. He's going to try to track you down, and he's going to use the route he expects you to take—the one that leads to Albany. That's why the last thing you can do is what he expects. He's not going to do anything dramatic except as a last resort; remember what he's got to lose. All we've got to do is keep him guessing, until . . ."

"Until what?" Cathy's voice was hoarse, scratchy. Her head was spinning, her thoughts racing like rats in a maze.

Dave didn't answer. He didn't know the answer, and the question was running through his head, over and over again, with pieces of the conversation he'd had with the chief, things that nagged at him, things he didn't understand, answers he didn't have. Until what? Until the FBI stepped in? He knew what their plan was, and he didn't like it. Until Kreiger, helpless without the information Cathy had in her head, stepped into a trap of his own making? Maybe, but Dave didn't like to stake his life on such a big maybe. Until Kreiger found them? That was more likely, and not a very appealing scenario either.

Cathy repeated, echoing his thoughts, "Until *what?*" Her voice was rising toward the edge of hysteria. "Until it all just goes away? What?"

It wasn't until that moment that Dave fully realized, or finally accepted, just how alone the two of them were. Help wasn't coming. They were completely on their own. And it was up to Dave whether they lived or died.

He answered, "Until I figure out what to do."

And he moved ahead of her down the hill.

Chapter Fourteen

Cathy did not go back into the cabin. She sat on the steps and stared out at the lake and wondered why, of all the torments she had endured in the past twenty-four hours, the waiting should be the hardest. And the worst was that she didn't even know what she was waiting for.

No, the worst was the pictures that kept flashing through her mind: Ellen, held captive and tortured for the sake of information she didn't possess; the twins, ruthlessly kidnaped from the hospital at gunpoint; Jack, lying helpless with tubes in his arms and machines breathing for him . . .

I can't stay here, she thought, over and over again. *I can't.*

The screen door slammed behind her, making her jump. Dave sat down beside her, placing a paper plate of toaster pastries between them, holding the handles of two coffee mugs in the other hand. He passed one of the cups to her and nodded toward the plate. "I warmed them up. You should eat."

Cathy knew he was right. She wasn't sure how much of the nausea that swept through her was from horror and exhaustion, and how much was simple hunger. She broke off a corner of a pastry and it tasted like cardboard in her mouth.

She took a swallow of coffee. "It's like," she said, as matter-of-factly as she could, "God is making up for all the times he let me slip by before. Nothing really bad has ever happened to me before, you know. Now all of a sudden, everything I care about is being torn apart, taken away. It's like one of those old-time Bible plagues."

"Job," Dave said.

Cathy looked at him questioningly.

"He was the character in the Bible who led a charmed life," Dave explained, "until God decided to teach him a lesson. That's where the expression 'the trials of Job' comes from." He returned his gaze to the lake. "My wife was all the time throwing things like that into the conversation."

Cathy dropped her gaze to the coffee cup. "I wondered."

"What?"

"Who the woman was who loved you."

Dave cast a quick surprised glance in her direction, then looked back at the lake. "She was a lot better than I deserved, I can tell you that much," he said after a moment.

"She's not with you anymore?"

There was a small silence, then he sipped his

215

coffee without looking at her. "Cancer. Eight years ago."

"I'm sorry."

Cathy warmed her hands around the coffee cup. Despite the ever-brightening day, there was a definite chill in the air. Or perhaps the chill came from inside her. She said quietly after a time, "What happened to him?"

"Who?"

"Job."

"I don't know. But I think that's also where the expression 'curse God and die' comes from."

Cathy glanced at him, but he wasn't smiling. She said dryly, "I never heard that one."

His expression was bleak and faraway. "I have."

Cathy looked away. They drank their coffee in silence for a while.

She broke off another corner of the pastry. "You're not eating."

"I hate those things." But he picked one up anyway, and bit into it.

Cathy said, "We're not leaving today, are we?"

He waited until he finished the pastry. "Kreiger killed a civilian back at the truck stop," he said. "Maybe by accident, maybe on purpose. But it's my description on the APB. And yours. Which means we couldn't take the car, even if we switched plates."

It took a long, long time for all of that to sink in. When it did, all Cathy could think of was how safe she had felt with him before this. There had been suspicion, there had been uncertainty, but beneath it all there had been a sense of rightness, of safety. He was one of the good guys, and he was on her side. Now he was in as much trouble as she was, and there was nothing either of them could do to help the other.

She didn't know what to say. There *was* nothing she could say. Dead ends, blank walls. The trap was closing. Ellen, Jack, the twins . . .

Dave said, "Time is on our side. Kreiger has a deadline. There are two crucial factors in a drug drop: the time and the place. We know he's missing at least one of those variables, and the longer we wait — "

"The more desperate he gets," Cathy said tightly. "Desperate enough to take the children, or Ellen. . . . Damn it, you're a cop! Is that the best plan you can think of? Isn't there something you can *do?*"

Cathy knew she had no right to take her fear and her anxiety out on him. She knew that it was because of her, and what he had done to help her, that his hands were now tied and he was as much of a fugitive as she was. She knew, too, that without him she never would have made it this far. She might not even have survived the night. But when she saw his jaw knot with impotence and frustration she didn't feel guilty for the unfairness of her accusations; she felt angry.

"I don't know," he said in a low, deliberate tone, "where you get your ideas about cops, but this isn't a goddamn TV series. I know about taking down statements and filling out reports and sitting on twelve-hour stakeouts waiting for nothing to happen. I *don't* know about matching wits with a trained killer and outsmarting half the government agencies in the Pacific Northwest, so if you're expecting me to come up with a quick happy ending for this little fairy tale, let me clue you in: it's not going to happen."

"I don't expect anything from you," she said, her voice shaking with emotion though she tried to keep it calm. "I expected someone to help me when I dialed 911, and instead you and your friend came looking to gun me down. I expected the officer who pulled me over on the freeway to listen to my story and give me some protection, but instead he arrested me and impounded my car and turned me over to the man who was trying to kill me. I even expected Kreiger to take me to my car and let me go, all because he showed me a badge—so what should I expect from *you?*"

She felt the tears backing up, tears of anger and frustration and self pity, and she hated them. She glanced at the coffee cup in her hand and started to take a sip, then abruptly tossed the contents over the rail. "Besides all that, you make a lousy cup of coffee."

She got to her feet, turning toward the cabin, not wanting to go in; but the tears were hot and thick and the emptiness inside her was so great that she had to do something.

Then Dave said, "I know." And she could hear the smile in his voice. "Alice suffered through five anniversaries of breakfast in bed before she finally told me the same thing. I guess she didn't want to hurt my feelings."

Cathy's shoulders slumped; she couldn't fight the tears anymore. "I can't do this by myself," she whispered.

He stood beside her, and when his arm came around her shoulders it seemed only natural, warm and strong. She wanted to lean on him, but she didn't dare. He turned her lightly in the circle of his arm so that she was facing his chest. He touched her chin, making her look at him, and he said soberly, "First of all, you *can* do this by yourself, if you have to. You've got more guts than any woman I've ever known, Cathy Hamilton."

She started to look away, disparaging his words, but he wouldn't let her. He held her gaze firmly, as though by the force of his mind he could impress on her the importance, the sincerity of his words; and in a way it worked. For a moment, she believed him.

"I mean it," he said. "When this whole thing started I gave you about a fifteen percent chance of survival, and that was when I thought you were a professional. You've made all the right moves, you anticipated everything that lay in front of you, you fought when you had to and you ran when you had to, and you've made it this far *by yourself*." And then his expression softened. "But you're not by yourself anymore. Not unless you want to be."

Cathy dropped her eyes. It felt good, being close to him, being surrounded by his strength, listening to him tell her things that she knew she shouldn't believe. She didn't want to lose the moment. She wanted to rest there, protected by him, to believe everything was going to be all right. But she said, "I was going to leave you last night. And today, if I could've gotten away . . ."

He said, "I know." He stepped away from her. "I should probably say I wouldn't try to stop you, but you know I would. Our chances don't look great in any case, but they're better together."

She clenched her fists slowly. "We can't just *sit* here, waiting for him to find us."

"He won't find us," Dave insisted firmly, "not unless one of us does something stupid. I figure a couple of days, max, before this whole thing is going to blow up in somebody's face."

He saw the anxiety build behind her eyes, and he forestalled her next protest with a deep breath. "Meanwhile, though," he said, "I've packed the backpack and filled the canteens. Around twilight we'll start hiking toward that little town down there. We should have plenty of time to make it before dark. Then we'll steal another car and drive it as far as we can. I told you I'd get you to Jack, and I will."

The thought of another nightmarish flight in a stolen car made Cathy feel ill, as though the very cells of her skin, sinew, and bone were rising up in protest. How could she go through that again? What choice did they have?

She said, struck by a sudden thought that she hoped was not as desperate as it sounded, "The

FBI. Why don't I just tell them what I know—what the man on the phone said? They know I'm not a criminal. If I cooperated, they would protect me—us."

Dave shook his head, starting to turn away. "That's not what they want from you. Chances are they know exactly what was said on the phone. What they want is for Kreiger to find out, and walk into their trap."

And then Dave stopped, and looked back at her, the light of a sudden cautious hope in his eyes.

"What?" she insisted.

The light faded, and he shook his head again. "Nothing. *They* may know what the code means, but we don't. Just letters and numbers."

"Damn it," Cathy cried, "the man has killed at least two people! Can't they stop him? What more do they need?"

A scrap of the morning's conversation with the chief flitted across Dave's consciousness, disturbing him; something that wasn't quite right, something he should have paid closer attention to . . . but it was gone. He gave Cathy a shrug and a bitter smile, and answered, "Just more, I guess."

He went into the cabin and returned in a moment with the gun she had taken from Kreiger. Cathy recoiled instinctively when she saw it. In the daylight, it looked even uglier and more lethal than it had last night.

He said, "There's a full clip, but that's the only ammunition we've got for this gun. The store

221

doesn't sell it, even if I wanted to risk buying it. So we're not going to waste a lot on target practice." He removed the clip, showed it to her just as though he expected her to recognize what she was seeing, and replaced it. "Come on around back."

He went down the steps, but Cathy hung back. He was almost around the side of the cabin before she followed.

"I can't believe that brother of yours never taught you to shoot." Dave's voice was casual as he moved through the high, ragged grass toward a rust-stained steel trash barrel.

"Not every man believes guns are the solution to violence," Cathy replied a little stuffily, but in her mind she was hearing Jack's voice. *Sometimes you've got to be prepared for the worst.*

Dave picked out a couple of tin cans, long since scoured clean by insects, and took them over to a stump. "That's right," he said, "he's an academic. Stands to reason he'd be a pacifist. The only trouble with pacifists—like academics—is they live in a world of their own. And all that happy bullshit they're always spouting about social reform being the only answer to the crime problem doesn't have a damn thing to do with what goes on in real life." He turned from setting up the cans, a mild challenge in his eyes. "Does it?"

Cathy frowned a little, disturbed and puzzled by the hostility she sensed beneath his words—hostility directed, for some unknown reason, at Jack. "Jack's not like that," she said. "And neither am I, if that's what you're implying."

"Of course not. You know that your average junkie on the street is not going to be interested in listening to reason when he's got you pinned against the wall with a knife at your throat. And you know a man like Kreiger doesn't spend a lot of his evenings reading papers on social change. And your brother would want you to be safe. That's why you're going to learn how to use this weapon, am I right?"

Cathy swallowed hard, staring at the gun in his hand. "It's no use. You were right last night—I can't use it, not on a man, not when it counts. If I could have, I would have used it on you."

Dave's expression was dry. "Not with the safety on, you wouldn't have—fortunately for me. And while I'm glad I was right about you last night, that's not a mistake you can afford to make again."

She shook her head. "No. You're the policeman, you carry the guns. I don't have to—"

"Yes, you do. Because even if you never have to fire this, you need the confidence of knowing you can." He placed the gun firmly in her hand, wrapping her fingers about it. And he held her gaze. "That's what I saw in your eyes last night—uncertainty. You don't ever want anybody else to see that, I promise you."

Her throat was dry. "You talk as though—" She almost didn't finish. She didn't want to finish, but he was looking at her, waiting. She flexed her hand uncomfortably around the butt of the pistol. "You're making it sound like I'm going to get a

223

chance to use this."

He said, "That's right."

"But a minute ago you said we were safe if we kept moving! Besides, if we stay together—"

"What do you want mē to say?" Dave replied impatiently. "Do you want me to tell you not to worry, that everything is going to be all right? That I'll take care of you and you don't have to be afraid? For Christ's sake, Cathy, you know better than that!"

Cathy realized that was exactly what she wanted him to do. That was what Jack would have done, what every man she had ever known would have done. And now, when she needed to hear those meaningless platitudes most, she had to depend upon the one man whose false impressions of her courage and common sense refused to allow him to say them. She knew she should be ennobled by that, but in fact she felt hurt and lost.

She said wearily, "I know. But I would have liked to hear it."

Dave looked a little surprised, and then uncomfortable, though his tone softened. "Look," he said, "I *hope* everything's going to be all right. I promise I'll take care of you—of us—the best I can. But I can't tell you not to worry. Okay?"

After a moment Cathy managed a slow, reluctant smile. "I just realized something," she said. "That's the first time anyone has talked to me like a grown-up in a long time. I guess it's okay. I might even learn to like it."

Dave looked at her a moment as though he did

not quite know whether or not she intended him to take her seriously, and then he gave a slight shake of his head. "Maybe some day you'll tell me who it was that taught you to believe in your own incompetence."

Resentment prickled, and she wanted to object to that, but she didn't quite know what to say. And perhaps there was a small part of her somewhere that even recognized a grain of truth in what he said, as much as she wanted to deny it.

At any rate, Dave gave her no time for argument. He was all business as he took the hand that held the pistol and lifted it into her line of vision. "This is the safety," he said. With his thumb, he pushed a small red button behind the trigger guard. "Now it's off." He moved the button back to its original position. "You keep it here until you're ready to pull the trigger, until there's absolutely no doubt that you're going to pull the trigger. All right?"

She nodded.

"Do it."

He moved his hand away and she moved the button forward, then back.

He stepped behind her, putting his hands under her arms as he moved them into position. "Put your feet apart. No, farther. Find your center of balance, be comfortable. Pretend like you're bracing against a big wind, that's it. This gun is too heavy for a woman, it's not going to be easy to handle. The best thing for you to do is hold it with both hands and brace your arms against something — a tabletop, a car hood, a rock, something to keep your arm from shaking. If you can't, hold the gun with your right hand and use the other hand to support your arm, like this." He positioned her left hand beneath her wrist. "Look down the sights. Get one of the cans centered."

She shook her head. The gun was still wavering, not much, but enough to keep the small tin can floating in and out of the frame of the sights. "I can never hit that. It's too small."

"Don't worry," he said calmly, "A man makes a much bigger target. And you're not even going to take the safety off until he's close enough to hit with a rock. Right?"

She swallowed hard. He made it sound like a game, and they both knew that was the last thing it was. He was talking about a real man, a man with a face and a name, a man who would bleed if a bullet tore through his flesh . . . a man who only last night would not have hesitated to use this very gun on Cathy if he had had the chance.

Dave was saying, "Now there's going to be a hell of a kick, but don't stiffen against it. Let your arms take the impact, stay as relaxed as you can. Squeeze the trigger, don't jerk it. Get your target in your sights and when you do, don't hesitate. Fire." He stepped away from her. "Go ahead."

"Do you mean now?"

"You need to get used to the feel. We'll take a couple of practice shots."

Cathy hated this; she hated the act and the reason for it, but she knew arguing with Dave would only prolong the inevitable. She knew she couldn't pull the trigger on another human being. Throughout the night she had physically fought for her life; she had used force when she had to, and it had sickened her, but it was a force she could control. A gun was different. Holding it had made her feel secure, pointing it made her feel powerful, and she liked that feeling. But she had known with horrible certainty when Dave approached her down the barrel of the gun that she couldn't pull the trigger, that she wouldn't pull the trigger no matter what the provocation. Firing a couple of shots at a rusty tin can was not going to change that basic truth.

But she didn't want to argue with Dave. She tensed her arms against the impact and squeezed her eyes shut even as she tried not to avert her face. She tugged on the trigger, and nothing happened.

Dave said, "Cathy."

She looked at him, but he said nothing more. He simply reached forward and flipped the safety button. His expression was bland but she knew he was disappointed, and that irritated her. She braced herself tightly and pulled the trigger.

The explosion was shattering; the recoil threw her arm up and sent her staggering backward. She didn't come close to the tin can, which wasn't surprising. She couldn't even remember whether she had glanced at the sights before she fired.

She had forgotten or ignored everything Dave

had told her, and she expected him to be angry. Instead, he took the gun from her hand, pushed the safety back on, and said mildly, "Most women don't like guns. They're loud, they're messy. My wife once said that if men had to worry about who was going to clean up the mess, there'd be a lot less violence in the world."

Cathy was ashamed. He had been trying to help her and she had deliberately, almost spitefully, ignored him. And instead of reproaching her or throwing his hands up in exasperation, he understood. He understood, in fact, a great deal better than Cathy would have done under the same circumstances.

She said, "Your wife sounds like a special person."

"She was." He said it matter of factly, without bitterness or wistfulness, a simple statement of fact.

Cathy thought he was somewhat special, too, but she didn't feel she knew him well enough to say so. She extended her hand for the gun instead. "Let me try it again."

He started to hand it to her, and then a sound tore across the day—almost an echo of the gunshot that had gone before; not as explosive, yet at the same time sharper, cleaner, more purposeful. Cathy didn't recognize it; she *refused* to recognize it; even when she saw the ragged shock on Dave's face as he shouted, "Get inside!" Even as he grabbed her arm and literally flung her toward the door, even as the sound came again and splintered the branch of the tree behind them, even as she dived for the door and even as she saw Dave running, low and close to the building, with the gun in his hand—she refused to believe what she knew it was.

She pressed herself against the inside wall of the shack, gasping and shaking, waiting for another gunshot—a bomb, a cannon, waiting for the world to end and thinking, *No, it can't be. Dave said he wouldn't find us. I believed him. It can't be.* She had been there less than thirty seconds when Dave burst in the back door. His face was pale and tight with urgency.

"He's about two hundred yards below us." He moved quickly across the room, throwing open a cupboard door and pulling out a moth-eaten blanket, a ratty-looking alpine sweater. "He must've been waiting for nightfall to move in. The shot probably made him think we'd spotted him. It'll take him about ten minutes to get up here." He spoke rapidly, stuffing the blanket into the backpack, tossing the sweater toward Cathy.

"But how could he?" she cried. She caught the sweater by instinct but immediately dropped it through clumsy fingers. "How could he find us? Nobody knew where we were, he couldn't have followed us, he *couldn't* have . . ."

Dave's lips tightened as he stuffed one of the pistols into the pack and the other into his belt. It came to him now, what he should have put together sooner, what the chief was trying to tell him. *Certain players are expendable. . . .* The chief had known where he was going. Everybody in the squad room knew about Dave's fishing shack, most of them had been here at one time or another. Now Kreiger knew, too. Because in an operation like this, certain players were expendable.

He scooped up his windbreaker and grabbed the pack. "Take that sweater," he commanded shortly, "you're going to need it tonight. Let's go."

He caught her arm and propelled her roughly before him through the door.

Chapter Fifteen

For the first twenty minutes Cathy was too breathless, too terrified and driven, to question or even think. Dave forged ahead of her along a narrow wooded trail, pushing back branches, tearing through brambles, and Cathy struggled to keep up with his long stride. After a time the trail became less distinct and seemed to disappear altogether in places. Her calf muscles strained as the climb grew more definite, and her lungs burned. Dave never even looked back to see if she was following. Sometimes it seemed he had forgotten she was there at all.

She was afraid to pause or turn around, afraid to see the form that was in pursuit, as though as long as she could not see him he might not be following. She even allowed herself to think that perhaps they *had* escaped unnoticed, and eventually she stopped holding herself rigid in expectation of the shotgun blast that would sever a tree limb over her head or explode the ground at her feet or send Dave pitching forward or rip through her spine.

And when the climb became so arduous that her dragged-in breaths were like staccato moans, when she was aflame with exertion and her leg muscles on the verge of spasm, she was confident enough to grasp the trunk of a sapling and gasp, "Stop! I can't — I can't go any farther. Need to rest."

Dave continued for several strides as though he hadn't heard her. When he turned the dark scowl on his face almost made Cathy shrink back, and then she realized it wasn't directed at her. He barely even saw her.

But he was breathing hard, too, and after a moment the angry preoccupation in his eyes faded. He took a few steps back toward her, unscrewing the lid of one of the canteens. Cathy's throat ached too badly with the effort at breathing to try to swallow, so she waved the canteen away. He took a drink, gazing back down the trail the way they had come.

Through the breaks in the trees a magnificent backdrop of rugged mountains could be seen, jagged peaks still snow-topped in places, mountain pools and streams glinting like strips of tinfoil in the valleys. The hiking trail they had been following was such a steep, winding ascent that by simply moving out of the cover of foliage they could look down on where they had been. When Cathy's breathing had steadied enough for her to speak, she managed, "Is he there? Can you see?"

Dave shook his head. "I don't see anything. That doesn't mean he's not there."

"Maybe he won't follow us. Maybe—"

"He saw where we were," Dave said harshly. "It'll take him maybe three minutes to toss the cabin. Then he'll start looking. Sooner or later he'll figure out which trail we took. All we can do is hope it's later."

His words went through her like the cold blade of a knife, and then she realized something else—belatedly, stupidly. "We're going up. We're not going toward town at all, we're going in the opposite direction!" Her voice rose as the significance of this sank in. "The town is on the other side of the mountain, so why did you bring us up here?"

Dave's jaw tightened and his gaze remained steadfast on the trail by which they had come.

Cathy took a step toward him. "How did Kreiger find us?" she demanded, horror and accusation sharpening her voice. "You said he couldn't find us, but he came right to you! He couldn't have gotten here any quicker if he'd had directions, and now you're leading me back into the wilderness, away from civilization, away from help—"

"You don't get it, do you?" Dave turned on her, his face contorted with a rage that on a man of his general mildness was shocking in its intensity. "You really don't goddamn get it!"

"I get that you lied to me!" Cathy screamed. "For all I know you've done nothing but lie to me from the beginning, and if you think I'm going to keep on following you across this mountain, waiting for you to lead me right to your friend—"

Even as she spoke she was turning away from him, ready to plunge back down the trail. He grabbed her arm and spun her around, shaking her hard. "We're cut off, don't you understand that?" he shouted. "We're on our own! You go back down that trail and you're going to walk right into his trap! You show up in town and he'll be on you within an hour. There's nobody you can call he can't find, no place you can go he doesn't know about, *nobody you can trust*. We're on our own!"

He punctuated the last sentence with a shake of her arm that was so hard her neck snapped back, and then he released her. For a moment Cathy was too stunned to react. She simply stared at him.

He stood there, breathing hard as he slowly tightened his fists against an enemy he couldn't see, and the rage and frustration that boiled in his eyes was a horrible thing to behold. And supporting it all was another emotion, one it took Cathy a moment to recognize: the bitterness of betrayal. And she understood.

She brought her hand to her throat, rubbing away a sudden tightness. She could still feel the bruising imprint of his fingers on her arm. "Who was it?" she said hoarsely. "Who told him?"

Dave drew a deep breath and expelled it through his teeth, as though with the gesture he could also expel the fury, the hopelessness, the hurt. It didn't work.

"Shit," he said softly. "He tried to warn me." He lifted his hat, blotting his damp brow with his sleeve. "Hell, I've been playing this game too long to get used to a whole new set of rules now."

Then he looked at Cathy. "It was my fault," he said simply. "I should've realized which way the wind was blowing, I should've seen it coming. I don't have any authority over you, I can't make you stay with me, and I sure as hell don't blame you for not trusting me. But I'm telling you, lady, you're in deep trouble. So am I. And right now, I can't see where it's going to end."

Cathy wasn't sure whether it was shame or sorrow that made her unable to meet his eyes. She swallowed hard and said, in a subdued tone, "You figured he'd try the trail that led into the valley, toward town, first."

"Maybe." He sounded uneasy, and his muscles were still tight. "Maybe he's got a course in tracking under his belt. Maybe he's clairvoyant. Maybe he *is* the goddamn Terminator. I don't know."

Hesitantly, Cathy reached for the canteen. "How can we know where this trail goes? What if it just ends at the top of a gorge or something?"

Dave slipped the straps of the backpack over his shoulders and handed her the canteen. Cathy drank, sparingly, as he took out a couple of maps from the backpack and spread them on the ground. One was a hiking map, an almost unreadable conglomerate of circular land contour lines, dotted lines, and wavy lines, marked upon occasion by the depiction of an evergreen. The other was a more recognizable road map. The first Dave had picked up at the general store that morning, the second he had brought from his car. He arranged the folds of both maps to the same section of southern Oregon. Cathy tried to control the painful constriction of her heart as she realized how far away she still was from Jack—far away, and on foot.

Dave said, after a time, "It's hard to tell, but it looks like we might not be completely up the creek. If we leave the trail here"—Cathy followed the course of his finger with a sinking heart—"and bear northeast until we pick up this logging road, it should take us right down here . . ." He consulted the road map. "I don't see a road number, do you?"

Cathy knelt and looked at the map, trying to match the reference points from the hiking map, but her eyes were caught by the numbers along the top and down the side of the map. Bold letters and numbers in single digits, and smaller sections running north to south, east to west.

"Coordinates," she said softly.

Dave looked at her questioningly, and Cathy sank back on her heels, stunned by how easily it all fell into place. "Of course," she repeated wonderingly. "Not a code at all. *Coordinates.*"

Every muscle in her body tensed with excitement as she turned to Dave. *"That's* what Kreiger needs to know—not the time, but the place. It doesn't matter *when,* don't you see—the when could be now, or two weeks from now, or two weeks *ago*—it doesn't matter who knows when, if no one knows *where.*"

"And the safest way to ensure that," Dave said, slowly picking up her line of reasoning—and her cautious excitement, "would be to make the drop from a plane. And to do that you'd need—"

"Coordinates," Cathy finished for him, on a muted note of triumph.

For a moment they simply looked at each other, conscious of the thrill of the breakthrough they had made, yet wondering what good the information could do them. Then Dave said slowly, *"That's* why . . ."

He looked at Cathy, and the surprised discovery in his eyes grew grim. "The FBI doesn't know where, either. They're counting on you to lead them there—or on Kreiger, to be more accurate. Plan A failed when you put their best man out of commission. In Plan B, their best man is the enemy."

Cathy's head was starting to ache at the temples, as if something heavy were pressing there. "I don't understand."

Dave said abruptly, "If we knew what those co-ordinates were, we could let the FBI know."

"But they're the ones who set me up, who sent Kreiger after us—"

His smile was brief, and as cold as the distant

237

mountain peaks. "But it was nothing personal. And the only way we can win this game might be to play by their rules. Let *them* set the trap while we lead Kreiger into it."

"Do you mean . . ." She felt herself growing cold. "Deliberately let Kreiger find us, and tell him what he wants to know?"

Dave shook his head sharply. "No. Staying alive means making sure Kreiger doesn't find us. But if we could lead him to where we want him . . ."

A thread of horror crept up Cathy's spine. "It sounds dangerous."

Dave's expression was grave. "It may be our only chance."

She knew then what he was thinking. How much did she trust him? Would she see this as a trap in itself? And it could be. The information in her head was worth thirty-three million dollars. People had killed for much, much less. Even nice people.

And so he waited, and didn't ask.

Cathy said calmly, "Nine oh double-u one five, four oh en oh two."

And she saw, reflected in the simple understanding in his eyes, everything about their relationship change and settle into certainty. It was a good moment; the only good and true moment she had known since the world started spinning out of control two days ago.

Then Dave turned to the backpack, and scrambled through one of the outer pockets until he found a pocket atlas. After a few moments searching, he released a low breath. "Makes sense," he murmured. "Looks like a place called Cave Springs. Less than a hundred miles from Portersville. Why else would something like this start out in a little place like that?"

Cathy said, "We can't reach it on foot."

He began to fold the maps. "No. What we've got to reach on foot is a telephone. If we start back down the mountain now I can guarantee you Kreiger's shotgun will see us before we see him. I say we keep climbing and try to stay ahead of him 'til we reach a public road."

Cathy was aware of just how frail that plan was. She was also aware of the alternative.

"Dave," she said.

There was some surprise in his eyes when he looked at her, and only then did she realize that it was the first time she had called him by his given name.

"What I said before . . ." She dropped her eyes uncomfortably and then forced herself to look at him again. "I've never really thought you were in league with him. I've always trusted you."

He just smiled, and replaced the maps in the pack. "I know that."

She knew that wasn't true, but thought it was nice of him to say it, and to forgive so easily. He must have seen the doubt in her eyes, because he said, "Last night, you could have run when that dog was after us. You had your chance, but you stayed and fought. Maybe you didn't save my life, but you saved an arm or a leg at least, and you probably wouldn't have done that for somebody you thought was out to do you in. Thanks, by the way."

He extended his hand to help her up, and after a moment she smiled. "You're right," she said. "Although I don't think I realized it until just now. And you're welcome."

She put her hand in his, and got to her feet.

By mid-afternoon it was obvious they were not going to reach any kind of road that day. The trail leveled off in high spruce country and even seemed to descend in places. Just when Cathy allowed herself to grow hopeful it came to an abrupt stop, in a clearing marked by the remnants of many a camper's fire. Dave picked up a smaller footpath — or perhaps it was an animal trail — and Cathy gave one last, longing look over her shoulder to the last vestiges of civilization. From now on there would be no chance of encountering other hikers, no hope of the comforting sound of a Forest Service jeep . . . and hopefully, less chance that a man with a gun was half-an-hour behind them. They were pioneers, as alone as the first people who had crossed that same terrain a hundred years ago — and just as vulnerable.

Though they were no longer noticeably climbing, the topography was rugged and deeply wooded, and the air was thin. Already the sunlight was being swallowed up by the trees as it sank slowly through the western sky, and the thought of spending the night unprotected in the woods terrified Cathy. When she thought of everything she had endured in the past forty-eight hours, the prospect of one night sleeping with rattlesnakes should not have reduced her to cowardice, but it did.

Dave said unexpectedly, "So how come you never got married?"

The nature of the question surprised her as much as the sound of his voice, for neither of them had spoken for some time, wrapped in their separate anxieties and dark dreads. Cathy glanced at him and knew without further explanation that the question was designed to distract her, almost as though Dave had read the course her worries were taking and was trying to head them off before they got out of hand. Cathy felt a brief wave of gratitude, along with a kind of comradeship she had never really known with any man besides Jack before.

She answered, balancing one hand against the trunk of a fir as she pulled herself up a small incline, "What makes you think I've never been married?"

He replied mildly, "Not hard to figure out. Somebody who's spent most her life taking care of her brother wouldn't have much time left over for a social life."

Cathy frowned. "What are you talking about? After Lydia left, it was only natural that I move in and take care of the kids. But I've hardly spent my life taking care of Jack. If anything, it was the other way around."

"So he'd like you to think."

Defensive instincts bristled, but before she could respond he went on, "Your friend Ellen said you went to Juilliard."

Her tone was restrained when she replied; she almost didn't reply at all. "That's right."

"I don't know much about music, but even I know you don't get into a school like that just because you want to."

"I suppose."

"But you ended up teaching music in a small-town high school."

"I didn't give up my shot at the big time because of Jack and the kids, if that's what you're suggesting."

"No." His voice was maddeningly even, matter-of-fact. "You never even *took* a shot at the big time. Maybe because you never had to, maybe because you were afraid to, maybe because someone, somehow, convinced you that it was your lot to spend the rest of your life playing second-best to Jack. *That's* what I'm suggesting."

He was ahead of her by less than a stride; in one angry lunge she caught up with him and moved ahead, blocking his way. "What the hell business is it of yours?" she demanded. Her breath was coming fast and hard, both from exertion and fury. "How dare you judge me or my brother! You don't know anything about it! Why are you doing this?"

And even as she spoke she knew her anger was generated in part—perhaps a great part—by the certain knowledge that he was right. She had never had the courage to try for a position with a real symphony, although she had always suspected she was good enough, because somewhere deep inside she was afraid of outshining Jack. He had chosen academia; so should she, in her own small fashion. By the same token she had never had the courage to do much of anything without Jack's approval, because he was her anchor, her stability, her protection. And when he was left alone with two small children to raise, it never occurred to Cathy that her brother might manage on his own; she stepped in because she owed it to him, because she felt it was her duty . . . because she needed him far more than he needed her.

Dave was right, and she hated him for it.

He said, calmly and deliberately, "Your brother has made you an emotional cripple. Maybe on purpose, maybe by accident. But you can't afford that kind of baggage right now, and neither can I. That's what makes it my business, and *that*'s why I'm doing this."

Cathy couldn't face him anymore, and she had no answer. She whirled around and pushed forward. She had gone only a few yards when his voice stopped her.

"She's in love with him, you know."

Cathy couldn't help it — she turned to stare at him. "Who?"

"Your friend Ellen is in love with Jack. You might have noticed — and so might he — if you hadn't been so busy taking care of him."

This time Cathy let him get ahead of her. And he was quite a bit ahead before she turned to follow.

They made a cold camp beneath a rocky outcrop in the sickly green twilight of late afternoon. Both were exhausted, physically and emotionally, and even Cathy could see — and sympathize with — the effort it took for Dave to make himself stop, knowing that any delay would only bring Kreiger closer. But it would be dangerous to move through the mountains at night, or to push themselves beyond the point of exhaustion. They would have to sleep in shifts, and start out again at first light.

They opened single-serving cans of beef stew and ate it cold on crackers. As hungry as she was, it tasted like paste to Cathy. Neither of them had said much since the harsh exchange that afternoon, but even though it seemed as though every time Dave opened his mouth he stirred up more raw emotions, systematically ripping away her protective shields until, soon, nothing would be left, Cathy could not resent him for it. Perhaps she was too scared, and too numb with exhaustion, to feel anything. Perhaps she sensed that his motives were to take her mind off their present, seemingly insurmountable difficulties, by forcing her to tackle unpleasant abstracts. Maybe she simply couldn't resent a man for telling the truth.

She pondered what he had said about Ellen and Jack, and though at first the very concept strained her credulity, gradually she began to see what she should have seen long ago, what it had taken Dave—a complete stranger—only one phone call to see. Ellen and Jack. She wasn't sure how she felt about it, but it was comforting to think about them, about home and normalcy and small puzzles and problems, when she was sitting on a cold hillside watching night fall and the threat of death creep closer. She wondered how Dave had known, and she thought that a man like that was worth knowing better.

They couldn't have a fire for fear of signaling the enemy, and as the last of the sunlight faded through the trees the air took on a distinct chill. Cathy had already donned the sweater Dave had insisted she take, and now she wrapped herself in one of the thin blankets. She was so tired her eyelids ached, but she did not see how she could sleep on the hard ground in temperatures like these.

Dave studied the map in the dying light. "Tomorrow should be mostly downhill. Cave Springs looks like it's not much more than seven or eight miles away as the crow flies. We should make it by noon, easy." He folded the map and put it back into the pack. "You get some sleep. I'll take first watch."

Cathy swallowed hard, suppressing a shiver that wasn't entirely from cold. It was hard to envision the future when every moment was an exercise in survival, but she knew tomorrow was not the end of the journey, and only the beginning of the real danger. Tomorrow they could only hope they lived long enough for Dave to place a phone call to the FBI. Tomorrow the quarry started leading the hunter into the trap. Tomorrow she became a willing pawn in war games that used real bullets. It was insane, all of it. And Dave expected her to sleep?

She sat up and said, "You didn't sleep last night; I did. I'll sit up for a while. That is, if you trust me."

He looked at her steadily for a long moment. And just when she was beginning to grow uncomfortable under his quiet, assessive gaze, he said, "Look, about what I said this afternoon . . . I know it was none of my business, and I know I had no right to butt in."

She started to protest but he overrode her quietly, firmly, and without raising his voice. "I just wanted you know," he said, "that there was another reason I did it. I admire you, and Jack is

246

wrong. *You*'re wrong. You're worth a hell of a lot more than either of you have ever given you credit for."

She didn't know what to say. She hardly knew how to feel. He admired her. Dave Jenks, who had dodged bullets, stolen a car, outwitted and outrun an assassin, and saved her life more than once in the past twenty-four hours . . . Dave Jenks, who could make a few phone calls and understand Cathy better than she understood herself, Dave Jenks whose quiet voice could calm her racing panic and make her believe, against all odds, who faced her shaking, inexperienced marksmanship without flinching and who had, from beginning to end, stayed one step ahead of the FBI, the DEA, and every local authority who threatened them . . . *he* admired *her*.

She didn't know what to say.

After a moment Dave took the other blanket, wrapped it around his shoulders, and stretched out on the ground, using the backpack as a pillow. "Wake me in a couple of hours," he said.

She managed, "I will."

The stillness of the mountains was rich and deep. Their presence had frightened away nearby wildlife, and not even the small movements of squirrels or birds broke the silence. The sky, filtered through the canopy of leaves, turned a deeper shade of indigo. Deep in her own thoughts, Cathy thought Dave was asleep. Then he spoke again.

"After my wife died," he said, "I started to drink. It got bad, and then it got worse. It was touch and go there for a good long while."

A warmth spread within Cathy that was simple and complete: sharing, understanding, comradeship. She did not ask why he had told her that. He had, almost from the moment of their first meeting, begun invading her most private self; now he was offering to her the same kind of vulnerability. She was not perfect and neither was he, but that was only part of the message. The rest of it was too intricate and fragile for Cathy to begin to examine now.

Neither did she ask what had happened; he had recovered, or was recovering. He had faced his demons, just as she must. And he had won.

What she did ask was, "Why?"

His voice came through the deepening twilight, thoughtful and quiet, more welcome than that of any friend she had ever known. "Anger, partly. Helplessness, mostly. Sometimes I think they're the same thing. You don't go into this line of work unless you've got some kind of hero complex, I guess, and when I came up against something I couldn't fix I didn't know how to handle it." His voice fell slightly. "Seems like since then all I've done is come up against things I couldn't fix. Until now." He injected firmness into his tone and, though she could not see, Cathy felt him turn to look at her. "This time it's going to be different."

Cathy strained to make out his features in the deepening shadows, and could not. "What makes you think so?"

"Because we're overdue." His voice was strong with quiet, understated confidence — not a matter for question, just a matter of fact. "Because this time, the good guys are going to win."

And so they did. The morning sun was behind her when Cathy burst into the hospital wing. Her clothes were filthy and torn, her hair matted, her face dirty, and she was well aware of the looks the nurses gave her. For just a moment she was self conscious, and then she heard voices, dear, sweet familiar voices. Christopher and Janie came barreling around the corner, calling, "Aunt Cathy! Aunt Cathy!" Their arms uplifted, their voices shrill, they were alive, unhurt, unchanged. . . . Her legs failed her and she dropped to her knees, opening her arms, gathering them to her and squeezing her eyes tightly closed against tears of wonder and gratitude as she inhaled the sweet warm fragrance of them. And then she looked up.

Jack was coming down the corridor, leaning heavily on an orderly, but walking. There was a white bandage around his head and he looked pale and drawn. He was wearing the blue plaid bathrobe she had given him for Christmas. The children were tugging at the hem of her shirt as she stood slowly and began to move toward him.

"Jack," she whispered.

She moved faster. She started to run. And then the orderly lifted his head, and she saw his face.

It was Kreiger, and he had a gun pressed to Jack's ribs.

"Cathy!"

Jack shouted the warning but it exploded into another sound, a horrible sound, a final sound. . . . And it wasn't Jack's voice at all, but another's, and it wasn't a shout but a whisper.

"Cathy!"

She awoke with a start. Dave was bending over her, his hand gripping her shoulder. When she drew in a ragged, stifled breath he immediately placed a finger across her lips to silence her. "Sound carries in this air," he said, very low. "Come here."

She was on her hands and knees, following him from beneath the shelter of the rock overhang, before she was even aware of moving. It was a dark, still, purplish night that made Cathy think at first that it was still evening. Her heart lurched with the fear that she had fallen asleep on guard duty, but then she remembered waking Dave, shivering as she lay down on the ground, thinking she would never sleep . . .

And then something penetrated her sleep-fogged brain, and she identified the smell at the same minute as Dave pointed out the distant flickering glow far down below them. Wood smoke. Someone had a campfire down the mountain.

250

"It could be hikers," she whispered.

He didn't answer.

"Why would he build a fire?" she insisted. "It gives away his position—"

"He knows we're not going to come down the mountain after him. Even if we did, he's a good two or three miles behind us and would have plenty of time to set a trap. And he doesn't know where we are. There's a chance we might not have seen him; why should he be uncomfortable on the chance that we would?"

Cathy's chest began to tighten. It made sense. The fire could still belong to campers . . . but it made sense. Until now, with this tangible evidence of pursuit, Cathy was unaware of how relatively safe she had felt all day. But he was down there. He was coming for them. There was no such thing as safe.

Dave began to gather up their belongings, stuffing the backpack. "We'd better move out while we've still got a head start. Going will be rough until daylight, but that's his morning fire and I'm willing to bet he won't linger over a second cup of coffee."

Her throat was dry, and her voice a little hoarse. "How long—before he catches up?"

She couldn't see his expression in the dark, which was probably just as well. If he was lying, she did not want to know.

"He won't catch up. Not until we want him to."

He stood up, slipping the straps of the pack over his shoulders. "You ready?"

For a moment Cathy did not move. Then she swallowed hard, nodded, and got to her feet.

Chapter Sixteen

An hour after dawn, it happened. Afterward Dave would reflect on the incredible twist of fortune that had taken them through some of the most treacherous country he had ever negotiated, in the near dark, yet turned on him in broad daylight with no warning whatsoever. When his foot first dislodged the loose dirt at the edge of the path he muffled a curse of minor irritation and expected to go to his knees; when the ground continued to crumble and nothing broke his fall, all he could feel was utter, outright astonishment.

He bounced off the side of a cliff he had not even known was there, and felt something tear in an excruciating burst of red-white pain inside his knee. He heard Cathy's scream through a distant roaring in his head. Blue, green, and the brown of tree trunks turned over and over before his eyes as he continued to fall. He hit another outcrop and the crushing pain knocked the breath out of his lungs. He flung out his arm and tried to catch a protruding root; his fingernails bent back like badly glued labels and the root broke away. He landed with an impact that exploded into grayness.

By the time Cathy reached him, slipping and sliding down the leaf-slick gorge, she was sobbing out loud. His body looked like a discarded sack of laundry where it had come to rest against the thick trunk of a tree, limp and unnaturally still. She practically tumbled the last fifty feet herself, and she was on her knees next to him, gripping his shoulders. "Dave! For God's sake, Dave!"

He was opening his eyes even as she screamed at him, and the relief that went through her sagged in her muscles and left her light-headed. But when she could focus again she noticed the deathly pallor of Dave's face and the shallow, guarded sound of his breathing. When he tried to sit up he went stiff with pain and his skin took on a greenish cast. He closed his eyes, limp again.

Cathy's heart was pounding, and her hands shook in rhythm with each beat, as she tried to think what to do, tried to remain calm. "How— badly are you hurt?" she managed, almost steadily. "Is anything broken?"

She could see the lacerations on his hands and arms, the scratches on his face. It was a moment before he replied. "My knee—is pretty banged up. I think I cracked a couple of ribs." He had to pause and get his breath. "Give me a minute. I'll be okay."

He had lost the backpack at some point during

the fall. Cathy went in search of it, fighting back desperation with every step. She found the pack halfway up the gorge, and when she returned with it the desperation had not lessened, but her mind was working clearly.

She wet the corner of one of the blankets with water from the canteen and used it to bathe Dave's wounds. She said, "I don't know much about making a travois, but I think I could put together some kind of sling out of these blankets that would get you back up the cliff. It's only a couple of hundred feet."

Dave shook his head. "I can walk it. Or crawl. I just have to get my breath back."

He reached for the canteen, but his hands were shaking so badly Cathy had to help him hold it. When he returned the canteen to her she watched anxiously as he braced his hands and tried to push himself to a sitting position. She put an arm around his shoulders and managed to help him get propped up against the tree trunk, but his face was shiny with sweat and he was gasping for breath from the effort. With a cold, sinking certainty Cathy knew he'd never make it back up the cliff under his own power. Perhaps not even with her help.

Cathy turned quickly and began shaking out the blankets, searching in the pack for a knife or another cutting edge. Dave said tightly, "Cathy, don't waste time. I can't—"

"It won't be very comfortable," she said, "but

it'll do the job. I'm stronger than I look. I can—"

"Cathy, listen to me."

"No." She managed to unravel one corner of the blanket and, strengthening her shoulders with anger, tore it the rest of the way. "I know what you're going to say. Some stupid macho thing about leaving you behind. Well I'm not going to do it, so you can just forget that. It was your crazy plan to trap Kreiger, remember, and you're not going to leave me alone to get myself killed." Her voice was thick and the tears were blinding. She made another vicious rip in the blanket. She swallowed back moisture and lifted her chin. "There's an audition for the Boston symphony next month, and I'm not going to miss it. Not everybody gets invited to audition for Boston, you know."

It was a long time before Dave replied. When he did, his voice was tired and strained with pain, but through it all Cathy imagined she could hear the remnants of a resigned smile. He said, "I know."

The best Cathy could do was fashion a harness, much like a mountain-climber's rig, that fastened under his shoulders and around his legs. She knotted the other two ends together into a kind of yoke that went around her waist. When he could, Dave helped her by pushing with his hands and his uninjured leg, but the journey was torturous for him. When he grayed out he was dead weight, and the climb was almost a straight forty-five degree angle. Cathy thought her back would break. She saw white spots before her eyes and at times she was on her hands and knees, pulling herself up by means of branches and rocks. Once she lost her balance and slid downward six feet before she could stop herself, Dave's weight dragging her back with every step she took forward. Dave did not regain consciousness after that.

At last, with a burst of energy that was beyond anything Cathy knew she possessed, she pulled Dave the last few feet onto the path. Then she collapsed on the ground beside him, every muscle in her body convulsing with exhaustion. She did not know how long she lay there in that stupor-like state, hardly breathing, not caring whether she ever moved again, and unable to tell one moment from the next. It was Dave's moan that finally aroused her, and she made herself sit up, shrugging the straps of the pack from around her shoulders. She took out the canteen and offered him water. He could only take a swallow, and when Cathy brought the canteen to her own lips most of the liquid spilled down her shirt.

The sun was high in the sky by the time Dave felt strong enough to be moved away from the cliff edge and into the sheltering shadow of the woods. By then Cathy was forced to admit what she must have surely known all along: he couldn't go any farther. Not today, not tomorrow. Even if they were somehow lucky enough to be bypassed by Kreiger, Dave was badly hurt and he needed help. She could not stay there forever.

He was conscious, but in tremendous pain. His breath was shallow and careful, and even Cathy knew a night or two sleeping on the ground could mean pneumonia for one in his condition. His knee had already swollen up tight against his jeans, and that leg was all but useless.

Neither of them talked about what must be done as Cathy went calmly, deliberately about the business of making him comfortable. She cleaned his wounds again and wrapped him in the remnants of both blankets. She made him eat a few crackers and drink some water. She swept away with her hands the debris that might attract bugs or hide snakes.

And then she burst out suddenly, "Why didn't you just kill him?"

Dave lay with his head and shoulders propped up against a tree trunk to ease his breathing, and even through his pain he looked surprised when she turned on him.

"You had the chance," she insisted, tightening her hands into fists. "Back at the truck stop, when he shot at us yesterday afternoon, and this morning when we saw his fire. . . . Why didn't you go after him? That's what policemen do, isn't it — kill people?"

"Yeah," he said slowly, breathing carefully. "I guess they do. But I always figured — that wasn't my job. To kill people. Because the line that separates me from Kreiger is thin enough as it is."

Her brief surge of bitterness and frustration was spent, and was now replaced by a wave of shame. Cathy knew what he meant. Hadn't she, only a handful of hours ago, pointed a gun at Dave and loved the feeling? But she hadn't pulled the trigger. Maybe, in the end, that was all that mattered.

She hoped so.

After a long moment of shallow, unsteady breathing, Dave added tiredly, "I don't know. I've been thinking for some time now that I'm in the wrong line of work."

Hesitantly Cathy lifted her eyes to him again. "Why don't you quit?"

Again, he seemed surprised by the question, and it was a moment before he answered. "I don't know." The reply seemed spoken as much to himself as to her. "I've always been a cop. Maybe—I guess maybe I was afraid to find out who I was without the badge."

And then the introspective mood was gone, and he focused on her. His tone was as matter of fact as he could make it. "If you just stay on the path, and keep the sun behind you, you should reach Cave Springs in another two or three hours. You'll probably pick up a logging road of some sort that's easier to follow, but if you miss it don't worry. Just keep the sun behind you. When the forest starts to clear out there'll be signs."

It was a moment before she could make her voice work. "If Kreiger stays on our trail he'll come right to you."

Dave tried to shake his head, then winced with the pain. "He won't see me back here in the woods. I'll be okay. Leave me a canteen and a couple of those pull-top cans of stew. And my gun."

"But you said—"

"In case I get a craving for rabbit for supper," he explained, his eyes never leaving hers.

She collected the things he had requested from the backpack and put them within easy reach. The last item was the hardest. She placed it in his hand.

And then she just stood there. She couldn't leave him. She just couldn't.

He winced as he made a movement beneath the blanket, and when he lifted his hand it was scattered with coins. "Change for the phone," he said.

That almost brought a smile from her. After all they had endured, she had almost gone off without the one thing that would save them both. She took the coins and pocketed them.

"Call Chief Hayforth, Portersville police," Dave said, still holding her eyes. "Tell him who you are and that you have a message for the FBI. He'll make sure they get it."

Cathy swallowed hard, and turned to pick up the pack and the remaining canteen. Three hours. Keep the sun behind her.

She couldn't do it.

Dave said soberly, "We've lost nearly two hours.

260

He can't be far behind now."

Cathy shrugged into the backpack. Her throat ached, and she couldn't look at him. "I'll be back as soon as I can."

She started quickly toward the path.

"Hey."

She had to look back.

He was smiling, weakly, but the sight of that smile gave her all the courage she needed. "If I don't see you," he said, "good luck on that audition."

Cathy drew in a sharp breath, but released it very calmly. "You'll see me," she said.

She adjusted the straps of the pack and walked away, lengthening her stride as she reached the path.

Dave waited until he could no longer hear her footsteps, and still he lay there, measuring the sound of his heartbeat, staring at the green-laced canopy of the sky. Not debating, merely thinking. Wondering, perhaps, if there were any last words for the man he once had been — or thought he was.

He lifted the gun and checked the clip, examining the chamber for dirt that might have accumulated during the fall. Then he tucked the pistol in his belt and began the arduous crawl toward the edge of the path, where he would lie in wait for Kreiger.

Chapter Seventeen

Three hours. Sun at her back. She couldn't do this. Whatever had made Cathy think she could? Several times she had tried to read the map, but she was afraid to stop walking long enough to study it, and after Dave's accident had proven just how untrustworthy this terrain was she was afraid to take her eyes off the path. She had no sense of direction, Jack had always told her so. She could get lost on the way to the grocery store. How was she supposed to find a logging road in this forest, much less a town?

She kept thinking about that audition. Jack had encouraged her to send a tape and résumé, saying it would be good for her profile when she was ready to start teaching on the university level. She had done it because she was used to taking Jack's advice, and because it was the Boston Symphony, after all. She had never expected to be invited to audition.

Yet when the invitation came there was a part of her that was secretly smug, privately unsurprised, even as the more overt part of her was shocked and amazed and, yes, frightened. An audition was hardly the same as a job, and certainly there was no guarantee that she would win a seat in one of the the most prestigious orchestras in the country. Merely to be invited to try was an honor beyond measure, but how could she set herself up for failure like that? How could she compete with the top musicians in the country? What made her think she had a chance, and how could she face the disappointment of losing? It was better not to know, sometimes, what one's limits were. As long as she never tested herself she could go on believing that she *might* have been good enough for Boston. It was really better not to know.

Jack had agreed with her. She would have less than a month to prepare a piece. It was a long, expensive trip, and the competition was fierce. Why set herself up for disappointment? She had a job, a home, a life she was happy with. She didn't need the heartache.

Jack had convinced her. She had not realized until just now how much she resented him for that.

Cathy glanced at her watch. There was a numb spot about the size of a football between her shoulder blades, and it seemed to be spreading. That worried her. Her feet burned and ached from a dozen, a hundred swelling blisters, and her legs throbbed. *Keep the sun behind you.* Two hours, maybe three.

She was not calling the FBI, or the Portersville Chief of Police. She was going to call the Forest Service, and they would send a rescue team. Then it would be over. She was tired, and she wasn't going to play stupid games anymore. She was going to do what she had to do to save one good man who had risked his life more than once for her, who did not deserve to be left behind wounded and alone in the middle of a hostile forest with a killer on his trail. . . . She was going to come back for him, and bring help, and if that was the last promise she kept it would be enough. Then it would be over.

She plodded away from the sun, wondering what her brother would think of her now. She doubted he would even recognize her.

Dave had never before been a man much given to introspection or analytical thought. Things happened, and he took them the best way he could, because wondering why would eventually drive a man crazy. But now, as he lay belly down on the leaf-carpeted forest floor, half-concealed by the rough-barked trunk of a spruce, waiting for the man he was going to kill—while he fought the waves of pain that rose and receded like water sloshing in a bathtub, while he struggled to hold on to consciousness until he broke into a cold sweat with the effort—he wondered what it was, really, that made the difference between himself and a man like Kreiger.

Some might say it was the decisions men made. Kreiger had chosen the easy way, but so had Dave, after his fashion, hanging on to a way of life, a job, an identity that no longer suited him — that perhaps never had — because he was too afraid to find out what else was out there. Dave was using his badge as a shield just as Kreiger was, and he wasn't being much more honest about it. That wasn't the difference.

It wasn't the ability to kill. Dave had learned that when he gunned down an innocent man in defense of his partner. Maybe the difference was, in part, what a man chose to kill for.

Dave was lying in ambush for a stranger, and when he raised his gun it would be a weapon of war, not defense. That would be a first for him. But he wasn't going to kill Kreiger because he was evil and Dave was good, or because Kreiger was wrong and Dave and the laws of the society he represented were right. He wasn't even going to kill in revenge for those Kreiger had killed, and caused to be killed, before. He was going to kill because he had no choice. Because the only chance Cathy Hamilton had for survival now was if he stopped playing by the rules.

It wasn't that he didn't trust her to make it to Cave Springs by herself. She had accomplished far more arduous tasks in the past two days. Nor did he doubt her ability to carry out their plan. It was just that the plan was doomed from the start, a hopeless, futile, desperately naïve course of action that was based upon his belief that law and order reigned supreme. He was trained to think in terms of getting the man, the goods, and the evidence, a three-way win, clean collar, and that was all that was important. Sometimes he forgot the cost, just like Frazier had, and Hayforth. But this time, the price was too high.

This time there would be no evidence, no goods, no clean conviction. This time, maybe a man called Delcastle would get away to deal again another day. This time, maybe it wasn't Dave's problem. But a woman named Cathy Hamilton had to live. *That* was his problem.

Yet even as he heard the footsteps approaching down the path, even as he steadied the pistol in both hands and tried to blink away the sweat, he couldn't help wondering if *this* was what made the difference. And he knew that in only a very few minutes he would find out.

He had positioned himself about six feet away from the footpath. The small rise on which he steadied his gun provided little cover, and if Kreiger happened to glance to the right Dave would be seen. Dave would get only one shot, and he had to make it before Kreiger grew parallel with him, before he spotted him, while he was still far enough away from Dave to aim for a killing wound but close enough to make it count. Kreiger was carrying a high-powered shotgun and at least one handgun; a leg wound would not stop him.

Dave was nauseous with the effort of fighting the pain, of controlling the breaths that stabbed at his lungs. Carefully, as silently as possible, he twisted his body around to face the approaching footsteps, biting his lower lip as spots danced before his eyes. The pain was a live thing, gnawing at him. His vision blurred, and this time blinking did not clear it.

He braced his hands, one atop the other as he had taught Cathy to do. He narrowed his eyes, trying to fix on the sights. The figure within them kept wavering. He dared not breathe. *Okay, Cathy Hamilton,* he thought, *this is the best I can do for you.* He squeezed off a shot.

And missed.

Kreiger swung around almost before the echo of the pistol fire had died, spotted Dave, and shot. The bullet that pounded into the upper part of his body caused more surprise than pain, and as he felt himself tumbling back down into the gorge the last thing he thought wistfully, was, *I would have liked to hear her play.*

Cathy was too far away to hear the gunshots, but even if she hadn't been she might not have recognized the sound. She was like a machine, arms and legs propelling her forward with no intelligent direction from her brain. She kept the sun behind her. She kept moving. She hardly realized when the path beneath her feet broadened into a dirt track, when the woods on either side began to thin and the weed-scattered track became wide enough and flat enough to almost be called a road. Her brain was swathed in fatigue, and all she could do was keep moving.

Something about a change in her surroundings brought her gradually back into focus. The landscape seemed stiller and flatter, the sun beat down on her shoulders without the protective screen of the trees overhead. And wasn't that, barely visible through a screen of high, wild bushes and saplings, the roof of a building? She moved faster.

The town had been literally set down in the middle of nowhere. The dirt road gave way to a piney, overgrown field that sloped down to a flat clearing; in the background was a magnificent sweep of mountains, and in the foreground a collection of clapboard buildings and unpaved roads that had long since seen their best days. There were no cars on the streets. No people in the yards. No signs of life in the windows.

At the edge of town, a good two hundred yards before the first cluster of buildings began, was a weather-rotted shack whose roof had almost collapsed. Swinging over the door by one nail was a sign that said, "CAVE SPRINGS" then the paint was so faded it was illegible, but the last word was "OFFICE."

Something made Cathy keep moving, even though the coldness in the pit of her stomach had spread all the way to her legs, making them feel like lead weights. Nothing moved. There was no sound but the wind rustling the trees and the bushes, occasionally rattling a loose shutter. Where were the people? Where was the noise, the activity, the *life?*

She felt as though she was walking through a movie set, and though she must have known the truth from the first moment she saw that sign swinging by a nail on the rotting building, she kept going, compelled by the same sort of fascination a tourist might indeed feel while moving through a Hollywood set. The sidewalks were made of boards, rotted through in places and shot through with weeds in others. Many of the buildings, she noticed, had false fronts — a two-story Victorian-looking hotel was, when viewed from the side, just a rectangular box with a facade no more than a board's width deep. There were watering troughs for horses, and hitching posts, and even a saloon with bat-wing doors. Lace curtains, rotted by moisture and feasted upon by rodents until they were little more than tattered shreds, fluttered through a broken window as though moved by an unseen hand. Cathy walked from one end of the town to the other, examining every detail with stunned, incredulous absorption, until the piney field began to take over again and there was nothing more to see.

There was no telephone here. This was a ghost town.

Still numb with disbelief, Cathy turned back the way she had come, and her foot nudged something half-buried in the dust. It was a painted board, and she picked up it, wiping away the dirt until she could read the faded letters.

CAVE SPRINGS. EST. 1872.

"No," she said out loud. Her fists tightened on the board as the rage and horror and the impotence swelled within her. She lifted the board and threw it as hard as she could toward the nearest deserted building.

"Noooooo!"

She didn't expect to hear footsteps. She didn't count on receiving any kind of forewarning. There was no need for him to take chances while searching for her; she had not tried to hide or keep her location secret, and she figured he must have been hiding in the hills for the past hour or so, watching her through high-powered binoculars, biding his time.

But even though she expected no warning, not from an expert like Kreiger, still she was startled, and could not suppress a stab of cold, raw fear when, with no sound or precursor at all, the bat-wing doors of the saloon swung open and he stood there, silhouetted in the doorway with his gun raised, less than twenty feet away from her.

The scene was so much like a clip from a bad western that Cathy felt a gurgle of laughter back up in her throat; she suppressed the hysteria with an effort. But when he moved forward out of the sunlight and she could look him in the eyes the coldness inside her stomach dissipated, and her heartbeat was normal.

Wolf, she thought. *That's what he reminds me of. A wolf.* And even more so now, with the shadows under his narrow eyes and the blond stubble bristling his cheeks. The forest had been no kinder to him than it had to Cathy and Dave, but she took little comfort from that fact.

He had a shotgun slung over his shoulder, but the weapon he held on her was a pistol. As she looked at him he smiled, and lowered it. "Hello again, Catherine," he said.

Cathy was sitting at a table in the center of the room. Most of the others were broken or over-turned; she had righted this one, dusted it off, and found a chair with all four legs. Her back-pack was on the table before her. Before Kreiger entered, she had been resting her head on it. Now she folded her hands atop the backpack and spoke in a voice that was so calm and detached it hardly sounded like her own.

271

"How did you find me?" she inquired. "Oh, I know you had inside help to get to Oregon. But once we took to the woods, how did you know which way we'd gone? How did you stay on our trail?"

His smile, cold as a dying sun, widened a fraction. "Our government spares no expense on the training of its agents. I've tracked trained killers through the jungles of South America; keeping up with you wasn't much of a problem. And of course, once you got here you made it easy for me. Any reason you chose to stop here?"

"I was tired," Cathy replied, and her voice reflected it. "Tired of running. On the map this looked like a town. But it was a camper's map. I guess hikers come here sometimes. Tourists."

He made a sound that might have been a chuckle. "Well, those are the breaks." He tucked his gun carefully into his shoulder holster and started toward the table. "Now I think it's time you and I had a talk."

Cathy reached into the outer pocket of the backpack and brought out the pistol. She held it in both hands, the way Dave had taught her, supporting her wrist on the table edge. "You probably shouldn't have put your gun away," she told him. "Don't come any closer. Please."

He registered no expression as he glanced at the gun, but he did stop moving. He said, "I guess your boyfriend has told you all kinds of nasty

272

things about me. Some of them might even be true. But that doesn't change the facts. You have the information I need and you're going to tell me. So put the gun down. Make it easy on yourself."

She said, "That's just what I'm going to do."

He shook his head. "I'm not going to kill you, you know that. It was the cop I was after. He could cause trouble for me, but you—all you can do is help. He's dead, by the way. So if you're expecting him to come bursting through the back door in the nick of time, don't."

Cathy's hands tightened convulsively on the butt of the weapon, but she didn't take her eyes off Kreiger. How strange it was. She felt nothing inside—not fear, not anxiety, not sorrow. Just a great, engulfing fatigue, a chasm of numbness.

Kreiger said, without changing his tone from the mild conversational one he had used from the beginning, "I said I wouldn't kill you. But I can hurt you. I'm an expert in hurting. You're going to tell me what was said in that phone call, you know you are, so let's just get it over with. Haven't you been through enough for something that isn't even any of your business? Do you really want to be a hero for *this?*"

"No," Cathy admitted slowly. Every word was an effort to speak. "I don't want to be any kind of hero. And you're right, it's none of my business. All I wanted to do was get to Albany. All I wanted to do was see my brother. But I saw two men die, I almost killed another. You had me arrested, you stole my car and my purse, you kept me away from my family." Her voice tightened, but her hands remained steady and dry around the butt of the pistol. "Now you tell me you've killed the only good man I've ever known, and I hate you for that, I hate you for all of it, but you know something? It's still none of my business. I know there's thirty million dollars' worth of dope out in the countryside somewhere, and I don't care. I don't care if you get it or the police get it or no one ever gets it. I'm just tired of it all. And that's why I'm not going to run anymore."

"Then tell me what you heard on the phone, and we'll part company."

"You'll kill me."

He shook his head, still smiling. "You watch too many movies. With that kind of money, I don't have to kill anybody. I can disappear forever."

"Maybe," she admitted slowly. "Maybe not. But if you came back, the police couldn't protect me. They couldn't protect my family. It would never be over."

"Why would I come back? Just talk to me, Cathy. Stop wasting time."

She said, mildly curious, "What if I don't remember?"

Still, no expression crossed his face. "Then I

guess both of us will be very unhappy. Now let's stop wasting time." He took a step toward her. "Put the gun down, and let's talk."

"No." Very carefully, Cathy slid from her chair and knelt on the floor, so that her line of vision was even with the sights of the gun and her wrists were braced on the table. Amusement flickered in Kreiger's eyes.

She thought sadly, *It's so much neater in fiction, Jack. So much easier.* And she realized with some surprise that Jack would not have known what to do then.

But she did.

Very carefully, Cathy pushed the button that released the safety. Kreiger followed the motion with his eyes. "I can't run anymore," she said. "I just want it to be over."

He took another step. His eyes were like chips of ice, and he wasn't smiling now. "Come on, Cathy, stop jerking me around. You're not going to shoot me. Put the goddamn gun down."

Let your arms take the impact . . .

He was eight or nine steps away from swiping out with his arm, snatching the gun from her.

Stay as relaxed as you can . . .

Seven steps now. The sights were steady.

He said, "I know you, lady. You can't pull the trigger. People like you never can. That's how come people like me always win."

Squeeze the trigger, don't jerk it . . .

275

Five steps.

Get your target in your sights, and when you do . . .

He was reaching toward her, a look of impatience and disgust on his face, when Cathy pulled the trigger. The impact of the bullet that severed Kreiger's aorta caused blood to spray the opposite wall, and as he died his eyes registered surprise.

The woman who was reflected in the plate glass window of Mercy Hospital in Albany, Oregon was pale and gaunt, bruised and hollow-eyed. Her clothes were rumpled and stained and her hair was wild and tangled around her shoulders. Against the backdrop of the night she looked like a refugee from the netherworld. It took Cathy a moment to recognize herself, and then it was with a dull and distant shock.

The uniformed policeman who opened the door for her was not Dave Jenks.

It had taken the FBI approximately forty-five minutes after she shot Kreiger to find her. The Forest Service rescue helicopter had taken another hour to find Dave. She had refused to talk to anyone, or to leave his side, until the Emergency Room surgeon told her he was going to be all right. Then she spent five-and-a-half hours in a small room that smelled like stale cigarette smoke telling her story to two FBI agents, wondering if there was any punishment strong enough to repay them for what they had put her through. All the time they had been less than an hour away, watching. She knew she should hate them for that, and one day she would, but at that time she had reached her limit of anger, had had her fill of hate. Until she stepped out of the patrolman's car a little after midnight and saw the quiet facade of Mercy Hospital before her, she was unable to feel much of anything at all.

She had talked to Ellen once during the ordeal, but had been unable to tell her much. Now Jack was waiting for her. She had made it.

A rush of cool, hospital-scented air met her as she stepped inside. The patrolman touched his hat and said, "I'll wait for you here, Miss Hamilton." She barely heard him.

Her sneakers made no sound on the tile floor as she crossed to the registration desk. A gray-haired woman behind the desk was reading a paperback book and looked up inquiringly when Cathy approached.

"My brother, Jack Hamilton, is here." she said. "He was in Critical Care. Which way?"

There was no fanfare, no victory march, no triumphant welcome to mark her arrival—just a sleepy-looking gray-haired lady who scrolled a computer screen, smiled absently, and said, "Take the first right and ask at the nurse's station. It's rather late for visitors, you know."

Cathy said, "I know."

She followed the woman's directions through the softly lit corridor until the nurse's station came into view. Two nurses were behind a desk, talking to a woman in a pink sweatshirt. The woman turned. It was Ellen.

Cathy stumbled the last few steps of the journey. Ellen ran, her arms open, and caught Cathy to her. For a moment neither woman spoke; they simply hugged each other fiercely, desperately, with all the strength they possessed.

Then Ellen pushed Cathy away, holding her shoulders, her eyes anxiously scanning her face, "My God, Cathy, we've been so worried! What happened? You look like hell! I couldn't make sense of anything you said on the phone, what—"

Cathy interrupted, "The children. Where are they?"

"It's all right," Ellen assured her. "It's so late, their grandmother took them back to the motel. They're doing fine, honey. She got here before I did and has been spoiling them rotten ever since. The old lady really does love them, even if she did try to take them back to Cincinnati. I wouldn't let her, of course."

Cathy pressed her face against Ellen's shoulder. That, and a tired smile, was all she could show of her gratitude just then. "Oh Ellen, I should've known you would come. That I could count on you."

"When I didn't hear from you, and you didn't

278

show up, I had to come. I had to see about the kids, and Jack needed someone with him, and I knew you'd want somebody to be here . . ."

Cathy looked up at her. "You," she said. "I wanted you here. And so did Jack."

Ellen looked confused for a moment, and then she smiled in shy, uncertain understanding.

Cathy said, "How is he?"

"Like I told you on the phone, getting stronger by the minute. They moved him to a private room not long after you called. Come on." She took Cathy's hand. "See for yourself."

Ellen pushed open the door of a dimly lit room, and Cathy stepped inside. Her brother, anchored by IV tubes and wearing a white gauze skullcap, lay on the bed bathed in the soft yellow glow of the nightlight. His face was darkly stubbled and his lips were pale, and there were bruised hollows beneath his eyes. But his breathing was strong and steady, and when Cathy approached the bed he sensed it, and opened his eyes.

"Hiya, kiddo," he murmured. "I've just been thinking about you."

Cathy took his hand in hers, closing her fingers on it firmly. Her throat thickened, and it was a moment before she could speak. "Yeah. Me too."

"Sorry — I missed the concert."

Cathy sat on the chair next to his bed, holding his hand against her cheek. "It was great."

"With you in charge, it had to be." His eyes

drifted closed, and he released a long sigh. "I'm kind of tired now, but later . . . we have a lot to talk about."

Cathy smiled, and slowly brought her face down to rest upon the pillow beside his. "Yes," she agreed softly. "We sure do."

Epilogue

Ellen said, "Are you sure you don't want me to drive you to the airport?"

And Jack added worriedly, "Maybe she'd better, Cath. You know how rattled you get in traffic . . ."

Cathy just grinned and lifted the strap of her bag onto her shoulder. "You two just stay here and take care of the kids so I don't have to worry about them. Tell them I'll bring them—no, don't tell them anything. Let it be a surprise."

Ellen had made sure the twins were down for their naps before it was time for Cathy to leave for the airport, thus avoiding tearful goodbyes. In helping Cathy while she cared for the convalescing Jack, Ellen had gradually assumed more and more of the duties that Cathy had once considered exclusively her own. And Cathy found that she liked it that way.

The two of them followed her to the front porch, Ellen carrying her violin case. Jack's hair had started to grow back but he still wore a red baseball cap for vanity's sake. Cathy had given it to him, because it reminded her of another cap worn by another man, and she liked to see him wear it.

Cathy took the violin case and hugged Ellen, then Jack. Then, in a burst of love and gratitude, she hugged them both again. She stood back, gnawing her underlip. "I don't know what we're all making such a big deal about. I'm not going to get it," she said.

"Probably not." Jack winked at her. "But then again, you might."

Cathy grinned. "You're right," she said. "I might."

They all embraced again to a chorus of "Good luck!" and "We'll miss you!" and "Drive carefully!" When Cathy glanced back after depositing her luggage in the trunk, they were standing on the porch with their arms around each other, smiling. She waved and they waved back, then went inside the house.

Cathy did not even notice the plain blue sedan that was parked at the curb until the driver's door opened and a man got out. He came slowly up the walk toward her. Cathy's heart began to pound.

He wasn't wearing his fishing cap, and the breeze ruffled his light brown curls. He looked younger than she remembered, even with the cane that helped him favor his right knee. The sun was in his eyes, making them crinkle at the edges, when he stopped before her. For a long time they just looked at each other.

She had visited him twice in the hospital, traveling the hundred miles between Jack's hospital room and his because she needed to see for herself, to know without a doubt, that he was all right. The torn ligaments in his knee would heal, but he had survived the bullet wound for two reasons: because Kreiger had used the handgun instead of the shotgun, and because simple disorientation had caused Dave to fall back down into the gorge, where Kreiger assumed he was dead or dying. Even now, when Cathy thought about it, she knew it was a miracle. But one for which they were both overdue.

The last time she had visited the room had been filled with policemen, and her presence had been awkward. There was so much she had wanted to say to him, but none of it was appropriate for that time and place. He had given her back her life, but he had given her so much more. How could she thank him for that? And later she began to worry that the things she had to say to him would never be appropriate, that they would only embarrass him, that he might not want to be reminded, any more than she did, of the nightmare of treachery and deceit that had brought them together. So she did not come again.

Now he had come to her.

He glanced at the violin case. "Off to Boston?"

She nodded. "The audition's tomorrow."

He smiled. "Good for you."

That smile, that voice, were the same as always. And as always, they made her feel strong inside.

She said, "You look good."

"Coming along."

His eyes lingered on her, and the expression there made her smile. He said, "You look different."

In her neat beige suit, with her hair tied back by a yellow scarf, she didn't just look different. She was almost unrecognizable.

She answered simply, "I am different."

He nodded, understanding. For a time nothing more needed to be said.

Then Dave dropped his eyes and said, a little awkwardly, "Listen, I don't know if they told you . . . they kept it out of the papers. . . . They found the drop, just where you said it was. They confiscated the stuff."

For a moment Cathy did not react at all, and then she shook her head slowly. "No. No one told me." She tried to muster a smile, but it faded almost before it began. "What do you know? Sometimes the good guys do win, after all."

Dave answered, "Yeah. Sometimes." But he wasn't smiling either.

The awkwardness Cathy had always dreaded would edge between them began to surface. She glanced away, trying to think of something to say. She wondered if it were possible that someone who had meant so much to her only a few weeks ago could have no place in her life now. He had created the woman she was today, but perhaps he preferred the woman she used to be. And in truth, they had never had anything in common at all . . .

She said, "Are you going to be out of work long?"

His smile turned rueful. "Well, about that . . . I decided to take an early retirement. Actually, we all felt it was the best thing to do."

Cathy found that she approved of the decision, as though it were hers to approve or disapprove. And she wasn't very surprised. "What are you going to do?"

"To tell the truth, I don't know. But I'm kind of looking forward to finding out."

Cathy smiled at him, and said, "When I get back from Boston—if I don't get the job—I'm going to start looking for my own place. Jack is almost fully recovered and—well, I think we both need to start building separate lives. We've had some long talks."

Dave said, "I'd like to meet Jack sometime. I feel like I owe him a lot."

"He owes you a lot," Cathy said. "And in a way—I think you already do know each other."

They smiled at each other, understanding and needing no words. It was a good moment, but it could not linger forever.

She lowered her eyes briefly. "Listen, I wanted to come see you, but I was afraid—"

"I know," he said quickly. "I understand. I thought maybe you wouldn't want to see me either, to be reminded—"

"No, that's not true, I'm okay with that—"

"I'm glad."

She took a breath, and met his eyes. "I think about you every single day."

He answered quietly, "Same here."

And then, after the longest time, there was nothing left to say.

Cathy glanced away reluctantly, and put her hand on the door handle. "Well. My flight is at three."

He nodded and took a step backward, balancing with his cane. "I'm glad I caught you before you left. It gave me a chance to wish you good luck."

"Thanks." She opened the door, then hesitated. "It was really great to see you."

"You, too."

She got in the car, and he closed her door for her. She arranged the violin case on the floor in front of the backseat and then started the engine. He still stood there by the door. She looked up at him. "Goodbye, Dave."

"Bye, Cathy."

She put the car in gear.

"Hey, Cathy?"

She stopped.

He leaned down to look in the window. "It's a long way to Boston. You want some company?"

Cathy smiled. For a long time she couldn't do anything but sit there and smile at him. Then she returned the gear shift to park, leaned across the seat, and opened the passenger door. "You bet," she said.

When he was settled beside her, looking at her and smiling, he commented simply, "Traffic should be light on the way to the airport. Good day for a flight."

Cathy nodded, sharing the smile, as she put the car back in gear and started out of the driveway. "It's a good day," she said, "for just about anything."